CRYSTAL SHADOWS,
GRIPPING NEW BLOOD

RJ PARKER

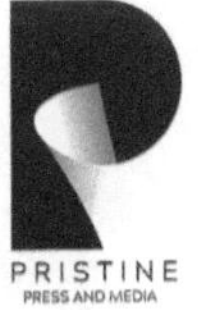

PRISTINE

PRESS AND MEDIA

Crystal Shadows, Gripping New Blood
Copyright © 2025 by RJ Parker

ISBN
978-1-964804-61-3 (Paperback)
978-1-964804-60-6 (eBook)
978-1-964804-62-0 (Hardcover)

CRYSTAL SHADOWS

VOLUME 1: GRIPPING NEW BLOOD

GRIPPING NEW BLOOD IS THE FIRST INSTALLMENT IN THE CRYSTAL SHADOWS SERIES.

My son, I fear that all is lost. The line has been broken, and no one will be left to fight the darkness. I know you tried, but it is out of both our hands. It was the best and worst thing that could happen when Sarah came. I have done all I could for you, and I can think of nothing else to be done. Raise her the best you can with the time we have left. It is coming just like it has ever since he woke, and there will be no guardians of our bloodline. Tell her when you can about us and how I died and stay alive for as long as possible. I lov…

TABLE OF CONTENTS

Crystal Shadows, Gripping New Blood

Volume 1

Chapter One

You Learn Something New Every Day

"Sarah! Hurry, or you'll be late for school!" her dad yelled from downstairs.

"Just a sec dad! I am printing my report!" She called down, not letting her focus stray from the computer screen.

"I thought you finished that already. You don't want to be a pro at-crastinating."

"Ha, Ha, very funny old man," Sarah yelled over her shoulder as her printer finished the last page. Even before the rollers released it, she pulled her paper out, thrust it into her bag, crumpling the pages, slung her backpack on, and dashed out of her room. Bounding down her stairs into their dining room, she grabbed a piece of toast and shoved it into her mouth. Her father was standing, holding their front door open, weaning his impervious look of not wanting to wait for her face.

Passing her dad, crumbs flew from his mouth as she mumbled, "Wet's goo, Dab, ow I'lw be wate." She padded his chest, leaving remnants of jam and bits of toast on his shirt, pulling his tie askew as she skipped out the door.

"Where would you get that idea?" He asked himself, straightening his tie in a mirror next to the front door, continually talking to her, raising his voice so she could hear him. "And why do all your pants have to look like that? Do all you fifteen-year-olds have to wear clothes with so many holes, cuts, and rips? It looks like some wild badger ate some of your pants for a midnight snack."

"Yes, Dad, wearing them is a rite of passage and bravery," she called back.

"The animal was probably driven mad by your music," he said, reaching for his keys, locked the front door, and slowly walked toward the driver's side of their new car.

"Ha, Ha, good one, senior citizen. When are you going to go senile, or did I miss it, or did you miss it?"

Her father unlocked the doors with a click and seated himself, adding an exaggerated groaning look as he saw her checking her appearance in the rearview mirror. She flipped her hair this way and that and, finishing with a wink to herself, before her father's hand blocked her view as he straightened the mirror for him to drive.

"Seriously?" she squealed, fastening her seatbelt. "Looks before books, Dad."

"Speaking of books," her father countered, lifting an eyebrow. "From a look at your grades, I can see that being a teacher isn't giving you any favoritism from my fellow pedagogues."

Sarah suddenly looked like she was struggling to suck through a plugged straw, saying through puckered lips, "Why don't we talk about that blackout we had a few days ago? Or that strange garbage workers' strike thing, or about those animals a few blocks away who suddenly lost all their fur? Why not the news of that family that said all their kids' toys came to life? Why you got to hit me with my clothes and grades so early in the morning, Dad?" She hastily added an overzealous smile.

"Why do you have to be like that? What's up? Did that guy with a big nose text you last night or something?" he asked.

"He does not have a big nose. Parts of his face are still growing into their prime. It's the new car, Dad. I can't wait to roll up in front of the school in this. It is really going to up my cred! Just the name of this sucker screams for attention. De Mazda CX- number 5."

"I have news for you," her dad said as he put his arm behind her seat and twisted around to watch as they backed out of the driveway. "I'm dropping you off a block away, and you can walk while I pull up in this silver werewolf killing machine."

"Dad…"

"It might help my students do better in class if they respect me more. Seeing me in this thing will turn a lot of heads."

"Dad…"

"I might just make principle yet, flashing this baby around."

"DAD!"

"All right," he said with a smile. "We will drive up together if you let me control the radio. I don't want to try to teach with a migraine again. Deal?"

"Deal, " she said, sounding calmer. On her way to school, she watched the houses give way to businesses. The radio distracted them both until a commercial sounded, and her dad turned it down.

"What's your paper that you waited for the last minute to print out, and who is it for?" He asked, risking a glance at her, taking his eyes off the road.

"Miss Amanda wanted us to write something special about ourselves. So, I wrote about how you, Grandpa, and I all have the same birthdays. I had difficulty finding stuff about Grandpa. I know she will want me to have proof, and I couldn't find much paperwork about him…"

"You don't want to find anything about him." Her dad said, sounding like all the fun was gone between them. Perhaps it was his change of attitude toward her that caused him to look at her differently, or just by happenstance he noticed her earrings.

"Where did you get those earrings?"

"Why do you care about my earrings? We were talking about my paper," Sarah protested. "You don't tell me anything other than we were born on the same day."

"Sarah, where did you get those?"

Sarah started to pick up on her father's anger before answering, "They are from mom's jewelry case."

"I don't want you going through your mother's things. They are not your things. They belong to your mother."

Was it the change in mood or the fact that Sarah felt hurt that her father was angry at her now? She didn't know. All she knew was that she was angry now, too.

"Do you not want me to know about Grandpa because you wanted to have a boy and didn't want me?"

"Sarah! That's enough." He hadn't raised his voice, nor did he sound angry anymore; he almost sounded pleading, as if he would be willing to do anything except talk more.

Neither spoke to each other, nor heard anything other than the radio until they pulled up to Christopher Lee High School. The sound of cars, parents, and students filled the parking lot as everyone enjoyed the warm weather. There was still an air of dampness from the storms they shared the past week.

As soon as the car was placed in park, Sarah unbuckled and pulled on the latch to leave. Before she could, her dad had reached for her shoulder.

"Sarah, please?" he pleaded, turning off the radio.

"Please leave your mother's things where they are. Also, learning any more about your grandfather will do no good. He did love you with all his heart. He would have done anything for you. He just wasn't given the time to live to show it, that's all."

"Then why don't we ever talk about him or Mom? Why all the mystery and secrets? Why do you keep that stuff in the attic that you never let me see?"

"Sarah." Her dad said calmly letting her go. Lowering his head, he stared at the steering wheel before saying, "I love you, and you know I wouldn't ever let anything happen to you if I could help it. Some things are better left in the dark."

Before he could say anything else, Sarah unlocked the door and stepped out. She gave her father a look that would crack glass before shutting the door and walking to her first class.

She left him sitting alone, not moving, not knowing what to say. The blue sky didn't mirror his gloomy mood until a loud group of kids crossing in front of the car caused his head to rise. Grabbing his briefcase, he rubbed his neck nervously. His hand stopped short before reaching for the door handle and asked himself, "Should I tell her? Is she ready? Would breaking the promise to her mother spare her pain or bring more?" Shaking his head, he said, "I just don't know. I don't know anymore."

Before he could ask himself any more questions, he left the car behind to teach his class. "*Work is the best remedy to get my mind off my troubles,*" he thought.

CHAPTER TWO

WAS THAT HERE WHEN WE MOVED IN?

The bell rang, easing Sarah's troubled stomach. She ached with hunger as she returned her book and computer to her bag.

"Sarah, please stay for a moment," Miss Amanda said over the other students' conversations and clamor. Some gave quiet Ohs and Ahs as Sarah rolled her eyes at her fellow student mocking her.

"Sarah," Miss Amanda said, crossing the classroom and sitting on the desk next to her, clasping her hands together in front of her. "Your report was good. Do you really have the same birthdays?"

"Yeah," Sarah answered as her teacher held her paper out for her to take. Miss Amanda always wore thin metal bracelets that complemented her outfit. "The only problem I see is that you didn't reference anything in it. You need something to support your claim, statements, and conclusion."

"Yeah, I guessed as much. My father and I thought you would say that." Sarah growled, taking her paper back and shoving it into her back with all the love of a used tissue.

"Really," Miss Amanda said. "Your dad was talking about me?"

"Uh," Sarah said, watching her teacher run a hand through her hair.

"Never mind, sorry," Miss Amanda said hastily.

Was there excitement in her voice for a moment?

"I want you to do your report again and cite your work by the end of the week. Then I will give you full credit."

"All right," Sarah said, readjusting her bag on her shoulder.

"When is your next game?" Miss Amanda asked, eager to change the subject.

"Thursday. We play Evans High." Sarah said as she started walking out.

"Good luck," Miss Amanda said as she turned to sit at her desk.

"We are going to need it," Sarah said under her breath. She hurried through the maze of kids in the hallway to the lunchroom. She joined her friends in their regular spots to get her food and tray.

"What took you so long," Rachael asked, fixing her napkin over her skirt.

"Miss Amanda," Sarah said, setting her tray down harder than usual, reflecting her mood.

"Ahh, Amanda, the bear huggin' panda," Shaw smirked, rocking in his seat slightly with a smile.

"What?!" Rachael, Sarah, and Jake asked together.

"Is she wearing one of her sweaters?" Shaw asked, letting his fork drop to the tray with a clunk. "She could wrap me up in her arms, wearing that sweater anytime. I mean, God bless the sheep that gave the wool that surrounds that teacher."

"And please bless those poor sweatshop kids who earned five cents a month making it for her too." Jack mocked Shaw's words, turning to his tray of food.

"Did she ask you to do it again?" Rachael asked. Both girls paid no attention to what the boys had said as if it were expected.

"Yes," Sarah said, taking a mouthful. "I have till the end of the week to get the references down. How am I supposed to do that when my dad won't help?"

"Just get evidence to back up what you have written," Rachael said, moving the last bit of food on her tray so it lined up perfectly to reflect six forkfuls.

"I know," Sarah said, eating fast now. "I just don't know how I will do that. Where am I supposed to find that info, a graveyard?"

"You worry too much," Shaw added easily while he ate, played a game on his phone, talked to them, and watched some cheerleaders across the room. "Doing a paper is like Anabel's hair over there. She has her hair. That is like the facts. Then she puts all that product in it. Those are the references you need to put in. She could be so hot that Burger King would hire her to flame-broil my burger with that smile of hers. But she didn't make the right references on her Burger King paper interview."

They all stopped eating and just examined Shaw as if they had never seen him before.

"She can do it," Jack said smartly, breaking their silence and taking their attention off of Shaw, who didn't seem to care how he was being examined. She has to keep her grades up, or she can't play on the team."

"Basketball, sweeeeet!" Shaw said smoothly, nodding, making his long hair bounce slightly.

"And if I don't, my dad will come down on me quicker than Mr. Lewis can put kids to sleep in his class." Moaned Sarah.

"Yeah, how is your dad?" Rachael asked smartly.

"And when can we hang out at your place?" Jack asked quickly. "My house is getting as dull as Mr. Lewis' class."

"We had a tiff this morning," Sarah said, taking more than a mouthful in frustration.

"Me too," Rachael and Jack said again simultaneously. They all shared a moment of wordless understanding between the three of them as Shaw kept sweeping his finger almost superhumanly on his phone while his eyes strained at the cheerleaders walking away from across the cafeteria.

"I don't get my dad's deal. He acts like inviting friends over is like releasing ten thousand mosquitos in the house or something." Sarah vented.

"I haven't really said anything nice to my mom in a week," Rachael said, finishing her meal, folding her napkin on the tray, and smoothing her dress.

"My mom is trying to relate again," Jack said hurriedly. "I just got a trio kill, and she just came in, didn't even knock, and sat asking what I was doing. Like, she would ever play Fortnite or know anything about it. Then she starts asking stuff like she is interested. It was odd, man, cringy."

"Parents. Can't live with them and can't have clean underwear without them," Shaw said dully again, wiping his long blonde bangs from his eyes.

"I just don't know where I will get the reference points. I'll just rewrite it again on something else." Sarah said, shaking her head and taking another bite.

"Amanda isn't going to take that." Shaw groaned. "She is one of those teachers that gives you all that, 'Oh, I believe in you. You can do it,' speech they learned in some class to make them feel better about what they put us through."

"What's the big deal anyway?" Jake asked. "Why can't you get the information?"

"My dad." Sarah sighed. "He is going for this whole Maze Runner thing where I'm not being told everything stuff. It's just me and him, and between the cabin fever without anyone else, he won't talk about my mom or my grandparents other than they are dead. I feel like I'm interrogating a P.O.W. All I'm given is a name, rank, and serial number."

"Completely relate. I always ask my dad for help with homework, and he looks at me like I am an alien or something." Shaw said.

"Shaw," Jake replied. "You don't do homework."

"Yeah, it's because of my dad," Shaw said, not caring. "He's the alien. No human would scratch themselves as much as he does."

"Homework is the best way to prepare for life after school and should not be unappreciated," Rachael said nobly as she stood up, taking her empty tray.

"You would," Sarah coughed, finishing the last bite of her food. "How many scholarships do you have lined up?"

"Not enough, and there is so much to do." Rachael groaned. "But if you need help tonight, I will gladly assist you."

"Nah, I will just have to face down the old man and tell him what's what." Sarah also got to her feet as the boys followed. "It's for a better grade. How can he say no to that? It's not like you are doing anything for Mr. Holmwood."

"You haven't been this way since that time you told me that a group of guys were after you when you were walking home, and they mysteriously disappeared," Rachael commented, putting her tray away in the dispensary.

Shaw's voice came from behind them both, "She has been making up stuff since I heard her dad asking why Monica freaked out over a spider in the classroom. He asked why she complained about the spiders coming into her home when it rained so much in that last storm. Honestly, you guys must not have any insects in your house." Shaw was shaking his head, putting his tray away as well. "What do you have to be afraid of?"

"No, Sarah!" Her dad said sharply over the dinner table. "That is final."

"Why are you acting like I'm adopted? Am I Darth Vader's daughter or something? Why don't you tell me?"

"Sarah, I will talk to Miss Amanda about it. You don't have to do the work. I will explain it to her."

"Dad, earrings are one thing. Not talking to me about family is another…"

"Enough!"

"Fine, Dad," Sarah said, straightening her back in her chair. The day turned to evening as she looked outside from their oval dinner table. They sat, not speaking to one another till both had finished their meal.

"Why are you taking your phone out?" Her dad asked. "You know the rule. No phones at the dinner table."

"All right," Sarah spat back. She stood up. "There. You happy? I'm not at the dinner table. I was texting Rachael. She is going through, like a drama, moment and needed my help."

"Well, since it's an emergency, by all means, save her life," her dad said with a fake smile, taking the dishes to the sink.

"Can I be excused?" Sarah asked, feeling guilty.

"Yes, you can be…" Her dad said, looking up from the sink out the kitchen window. He didn't finish because Sarah had already left before he could continue.

Time passed as Sarah took care of her chores for her part of the house. It had always been just her and her father. She never knew her mother and didn't know what having one would be like. She imagined she would not have to do so much laundry or vacuum if she had a mother. It wasn't so bad either, as their house wasn't the biggest. Most of their time was spent in their own parts of the home. All the bedrooms were on the second floor. The main floor was open, with the front door opening to a front room next to the dining room that connected to the kitchen. The television room was on the far side of that, which they never used. Going up the stairs, the first door to the right was her room. Across from her was a storage room next to her father's study and then his room.

She was all right, taking care of her half of the work. Rachael, Shaw, and Jake also came from single-parent homes, so she never saw any point in having both parents. Her father and she always made things work, so why should they change? But something about this recent argument bothered her more than usual, but she couldn't quite put her finger on why. Maybe it was because they always talked and never kept anything hidden before this.

Finishing her chores, she found herself in her room doing her homework more by routine than purpose, not really thinking about what she was doing. A knock on the door brought her mind to the here and now.

"Come in," Sarah called. "If you have to." She said so low that only she could hear.

"Sarah, what's wrong?" Her dad asked as he took a seat on the bed.

Sarah turned from her desk to face him but looked at the floor. "Nothing," she lied with a shrug.

"Look, I'm here for you if you need me." Her dad said, adding a genuine smile.

"Yeah, I know."

They both sat there, not saying anything. The night was coming, and the sky was turning red and orange outside her window.

"I need to go to a meeting tonight, all right," her dad said, standing up slowly with a strange look on his face. Was it disappointment? She didn't know.

"Can we talk about this tomorrow?"

"What is there to talk about?" Sarah asked, returning to her desk and lowering her head to her homework.

She heard her father walk away, but his footsteps stopped at her doorway. He must be just standing there looking at her. Why did he have to do that? She didn't look up back at him. She stared at her computer and paper in front of her like she was working but couldn't read a word.

"Just think about it, please?" he asked in a soft voice.

"OK" she replied like a robot.

"Love you," he said, still standing there.

"OK," she called back, still looking straight ahead. He didn't move. "Anything else?" She blurted, not giving him time to respond, "Because if you are not going to talk to all my teachers and get me out of work, then I need to get this done."

"No," he said. He sounded sad, as if his head was lowered. "See you in the morning." Shutting the door for her, he said, "Good night."

She didn't say anything back. She tried to read what was in front of her, but nothing made sense. She must have read the same paragraph five times, yet nothing stayed in her head other than the question, why? Why wouldn't he tell me what was happening with my mom and Grandfather? Was she adopted? Did her mom die in childbirth, and he blamed her? Why couldn't she know anything about them? What was the big secret?

"Ahhhhhhhhhhhh," She groaned and pushed her chair away from her desk. She spun her chair around her room. She was not looking at her television, printer, pictures of friends on her walls, or souvenirs from vacations with her dad. Each was a testament to the time they traveled all over. She had been to thirty-two states in America. Parts of South America, Europe, England, Scotland, and Ireland five times. They went everywhere together except for one time. She stayed in Italy for a week with people she didn't know while her dad was away. He said it was for business, and she didn't know any better at the time to care.

Her phone buzzed, startling her. Grabbing it, she saw that Rachael had texted her. "Did your dad crack?" she asked.

"No," she typed back. "He said he would talk to Amanda for me and get me out of it."

Rachael didn't reply. She must be texting someone else. The faint sound of the front door opening and closing took her eyes away from her phone to her closed door. She watched her dad in her mind as she listened to him pull out of the driveway, and was gone.

Now that she was alone, she felt like her stomach had hit rock bottom. Wishing for any relief she checked her phone again. Nothing. Rachael hidden written back.

"Is it that bad?" she texted Rachael. She waited for five minutes with no reply. She couldn't ask Jake or Shaw what they thought. She didn't want to know what they thought, and they didn't even know what they thought. She threw her phone on the bed and instinctively turned on her television, switching it on to anything that would be on. Just grateful for any distraction spinning in her chair looking at nothing.

"Listen to them, the children of the night. What music they make!" The television sounded. Finding that she was looking out the window at nothing made her take up her phone again. She just held it for a moment before sending another text.

"What should I do about my assignment?" She sent it to Shaw. Shaw was typing back.

"Murphy's law girl. If you can't get the info you need, then it needs to be made up."

"What is that supposed to mean?" She asked herself. "*He wants me to make stuff up?*" She thought.

"Cheat?" She texted back.

"It is a well-honored tradition carried on by countless generations of our brothers and sisters in arms against the educating instructors who would oppress us." Shaw texted back.

Sarah had barely finished reading it when he sent, "If you don't mind, a noob is trying to keep me from the Viking King achieve, so can we dispense with the obvious and stop the worrying. C ya tomo."

"I can't cheat," Sarah said into the phone with no one listening. "My dad would kill me."

She started to pace in her room.

"I hope you will find this comfortable," Dracula said on the television.

"Thanks, it looks very inviting, ouch." Renfield cried.

"Really?" Sarah smirked.

"Oh, it's nothing serious, just a small cut from that paper clip."

Sarah turned off the television and searched Google for other alternative facts. She was no more than five minutes in when she heard something downstairs.

"*That was odd?*" She thought. No one was supposed to be home. After looking at her closed door, she figured it was the wind or something and went back to work.

The sound of a clack scrape came from somewhere downstairs and again from the attic.

Jumping from her chair, she fumbled her phone and was about to call 911. Then, there was a knock on her door that made her jump. Before she could answer, it was flung open.

"Sarah," her dad called, breathing heavily and leaning on her door frame.

"I forgot something. I need to take care of it really fast. So just stay in your room, and I will head back to my meeting."

"Dad?"

"It's all right. Sorry, I startled you. Just stay here, and I will be out of here." He added with a tired, weary smile.

"Why are you going all, House with a Clock in Its Wall's Dad?"

"I'm not," her dad gasped, still out of air. "Just need a minute. Stay here," and he shut the door before she could reply.

"Sheesh!" Sarah blew, shaking her head. Her dad had never done anything like this. She listened intently, hearing nothing told her that her dad was still outside the door. She walked over to her computer, pushed her chair in without sitting, and started hitting random keys while still looking at the door. Then came the faint sounds of her dad's footsteps faded down the hall and the stairs. As quietly as possible, she went to her door and cracked it open, peering to see her father's head disappear. She carefully took her shoes off and followed, keeping quiet and low. It sounded like he was in the kitchen. She crouched down on all fours before lying flat on her stomach to peer through the posts and beginning handrail to see what her dad was doing without being detected.

He was bent over with his head in the refrigerator, so hastily gathering things that he fumbled and dropped several items, cursing his clumsiness. It was difficult for her to determine what he was awkwardly doing as the only light downstairs came from inside the fridge. As he turned around, the light no longer surrounded him but showed his side. She saw he had taken out lunch meat, frozen meatballs, a leftover roast, and four jars of peanut butter. He pulled them all together in his arms and on a plate, balancing them like a seal with a ball on its nose. He even put one jar under his chin as he gingerly walked to a bookcase at the bottom of the stairs. As quickly as he could, without dropping anything, he set two jars of peanut butter down to free up his right hand, moved some books, and felt for something behind them. It was difficult for him when suddenly there was a click. Sighing in relief, he returned the books and gathered the food again, resuming his balancing act. Sarah heard something click and slide behind her down the hallway. It must have come from her father's study.

Her attention and focus were behind her, where she had turned her head to investigate where the noise had come from. Looking forward again, she saw her dad ineptly climbing the first two stairs. Panicking, she crawled backward toward her room as quickly and quietly as possible. She was going back to her room, but she realized she had left the light on. Her dad would find her if she opened the door when the light would spill into the hallway. She scurried like a mouse backward to her father's room. His door was open, and she made it just in time to be safely out of his view before his head appeared in the hallway. She peered through the gap in the door and the frame and watched him come up and pause before her closed door.

What if he goes in or knocks? It looked like he was trying to readjust his load to free up a hand to reach for her doorknob. Thinking fast, she swiped her phone to link with her speakers and frantically hit play. "Play, play, play anything!" she pleaded to herself before, down the hallway, she heard the song 'Sweet Child O' Mine' from Guns N' Roses from her room.

"No! No! No! No! No!" Sarah pleaded to her phone. "What!? How!? You stupid phone!" She stuck her head out around the door while still lying on the floor. Her father looked confused about her music selection, obviously questioning if she was trying to send a message through her music. Then, shrugging, he renewed his arm-filed balancing act, and she watched him go into his study, shutting the door quietly with his foot behind him.

Sarah slowly got to her feet, crossed the hall on her toes, and listened at the door of her father's study. *Knock, slide, clunk, slide, scrape* sounded from the study.

"I'm sorry," her dad said, seeming as if he were in some farther closet in the room that didn't exist. I got caught up in going to a meeting and forgot. This should keep you going for a while. Eat up."

Sarah backed from the door in horror. Someone or something was in there with her father, and he knew about it. She looked down and found her hands shaking.

"I will check on you later. I have to go." Her dad called. *Scrape, slide, clunk, slide.* Sarah whipped around, not knowing what to do. Instinctively, she ran to her room, not thinking of the noise or light, and shut the door behind her. Leaning up against it as if there was an intruder on the other side, she dropped down to the floor, crying silently. Her father's footsteps came with the sound of his study door closing and were coming closer. She hurried, whipping her tears away.

"Knock, knock," her dad called as he wrapped his knuckle on the door.

She jumped up and sat behind her computer. He opened the door without her permission, a smile on his face instead of the open mouth straining for air to fill his lungs that he had before.

"Can you turn that down?" he asked.

"What down?" Sarah queried, not thinking, feeling the tears in her eyes well up still.

"That music," her father replied stupidly.

"Oh, yeah." She said quickly not facing him. She tried to work on her phone but to no avail. She couldn't get it to stop.

"All thumbs," she said as she crossed the room to the shelve with her speaker on it and turned down the volume all the way, still not facing him.

"You all right?" Her dad asked in a new tone.

"Oh, yes, fine." She lied, giving a fake smile, and faced him for the first time since he opened the door. "Why?" When she saw him, she half expected to see his arms still full of food.

"No reason, just…?" Her dad said, not finishing his sentence as if he were looking around the room to give him the right words.

"Why did you take your shoes off?" He asked suddenly, noticing them by the door.

"Oh, those," she cried. "Uh, school thing, you know. Study of, ah, feet size compared to, ah eating habits and ring finger size. Yeah, uh what size are you by the way, and how many calories do you eat, uh Dad?"

"Wait, what are we talking about?" He asked.

"I don't know. What are you talking about?"

"That's what I asked!" He said, straightening up the look of confusion increasing.

"That's right."

Both looked at one another, confused, compounding the increasing tension. Her phone dinged, indicating she had a text, making them both jump.

"I have to go to my meeting. See you in the morning."

"Yeah, morning," she said, swinging her arms back and forth looking very oddly as she struggled to ease the pressure she felt growing in her.

"Are you going to get that?" her father asked, straightening his tie and flattening his shirt.

"Get what?"

"Your phone," her dad said as he was about to walk out. "You got a text."

"Yes, Oh, you know, I will get around to it."

With one final look of confusion, her dad left, humming the words to Sweet Child O' Mine as he left the house and her.

CHAPTER THREE

IT'S NOT A PARTY UNLESS THE COPS COME.

"**P**ick up the phone! Pick up, please!" Sarah pleaded to the ringtones of her phone as she frantically paced in her room.

"Salutations, greetings, and felicitation. This is Rachael. Please leave a detailed message at the tone." *Beep*!

"Rachael, pick up, please! I am really going through something right now. I'm talkin' movie-level The Sentinel or Signs here, and I need you to call me now! Please! Now! Answer the phone! Oh." *Click*.

She hurried with her phone once more and called again. It rang and rang just as it had before: "Yeah, this is Shaw. Leave a mess, or don't. I don't even know how to check messages until later, whoever you are."

"Shaw, you idiot! Call me, or I will tell everyone that you still wear a Batman pajama onesie or something else I can make up involving stuffed animals and thumb-sucking during the daytime, right?"

She ended the call so hard that it was surprising her screen hadn't cracked. She parted her curtain and peered up and down the neighbors' yards as if a terrorist had been seen in her neighborhood and was lurking behind every corner or shadow.

She dialed once more as quickly as she could, keeping one eye on the phone and the other searching outside.

"Come on, please."

"Hey," came a boy's voice.

"Jack! Hhhhha, thank you for answering!"

"Isn't that what you do when you hear the phone ring?"

Holding her phone a foot away from her mouth, she shouted, "Will you just shut up and listen to me?! I'm in trouble here, you idiot! There is something in my house!"

"What do you mean? Like a table, chair, toilet, or fruit snack?

"No stup! Like someone, not something!"

What do you mean, A ROBBER?" Jack asked, panicking.

"No, no, no, it's not like an intruder," She squealed in frustration, feeling her hands shaking.

"It's like, it's, well, I don't know, but there is something in here and it, it, it likes peanut butter, peanut butter Jack. And it's eating all our food."

"Sarah."

"I don't know what to do!"

"Sarah!"

"What am I going to do when it eats all my father could carry and breaks out of there and comes after me? I don't have any sandwich condiments!"

"SARAH!"

"WHAT?" She shouted back.

"Uh, did that Statoski kid give you anything to drink after school, or did you smell anything in science class that you weren't supposed to?" Jack asked more casually, worrying about her reaction rather than her response.

"No, no, no," Sarah said, crying now.

"There is something, someone here, and I don't know what to do. Help please, help please."

"OK, where are you?" Jack said, now sounding severe.

"I'm at home and distraught! Where do you think I am calling from?" It was amazing how quickly Sarah could change from sounding scared and alone to angry and corrective.

Being more careful with his words, Jack asked slowly, "OK, where are you in your home?"

"In my room."

"And where is the dog, monster, peanut butter eating thing?"

"In my dad's office somewhere, I think."

"Stay in your room," Jack ordered quickly. "I will do it. I'm going to do it. Just block that door and keep it shut. It's time to man up. Don't come out, OK? Just stay safe. It's time." *Click.*

"Jack? Jack?!" Sarah pleaded to a disconnected phone line, crying again. She dialed his number again and again with no answer. A car drove by, scaring her. The world suddenly seemed changed. There was danger everywhere. Everything was threatening now. After trying Jack for a third time with no success, she tossed her phone down on her bed. Grabbing her shaking hands to keep them still, she searched her room as if this was the first time she had ever been in it.

"All right, uh," she said to herself. "The desk," she blurted as she pushed it in front of her door. With each minute, she found something rudimentary to block the door and kept at it until everything in her room was piled up in a mound in front of it. She sat on the floor holding her knees, rocking back and forth in the silence, now holding her phone, which was the only thing not in the barricaded pile behind her.

Her phone dinged, indicating a text. Sarah screamed in shock and accidentally threw it. She had thrown it over her head in somewhere between every stitch of clothing she owned and her books on the left side of the pile. She hesitated to retrieve it for a moment, then slowly searched, digging. Her hand barely touched it when it dinged again. She let out a small squeak and jumped back. Stomping her foot at how silly she was acting, she grabbed her phone and read.

"Sarah, are you safe? We will be there in a minute!" It was from Jack. She scrolled down. The second text was from her dad.

"Sarah, what is going on? I just got a call from the police and will be there soon. Wait, I have another call."

"The police?" All the blood drained from Sarah's brain. "He wouldn't!?" she said to herself.

Sirens sounded in the distance as two police cars skidded to a halt in front of her house.

"He would," she groaned, shrugging.

"Mr. Dexter, do you know the consequences of a fake emergency call?" A uniformed officer demanded, standing with his hand resting on his belt.

"Uh," is all Jack could get out. The strobing red and blue lights of the police car on the road brought far away onlookers to watch.

"It's a class one misdemeanor and a one thousand-dollar fine, you little…" The officer was cut off by her younger partner's hand on his shoulder.

"Easy," she counseled, stepping forward. "They're just kids."

The first older officer turned on his younger ward, "You can't be soft on these cell phone, recording, over entertained, self-absorbed, disrespectful, younger generational kids whose only answer to change a tire is to call a tow service."

Jake, looking confused, answered, addressing the younger officer, "I was trying to help."

The younger officer found her strength and stance that could hold the other officer back as he went off, "Liten you an undefinable person who need police to hand you tissues for something you can record to tweet at. You play in a world where no one can lose, where everyone is winners, yeah! There is no law so you can do whatever you want."

"Is this good cop, substandard unmedicated cop night, or should I ask if your captain ate all the donuts in the breakroom?" Jack asked hesitantly, then cracked a weak smile.

"You trying to be funny, couch kisser who has only seen the sun through a computer screen?" The male officer grunted while the other officer still held him back as he struggled to advance on Jack. "Why, you little…"

Pushing her partner back, she ordered, "Back off."

Even with her pointer finger at his chest, the male officer stepped back, muttering, "All right, all right, but one of these days, I'll see you, boy, without your overpriced stylist haircut."

Sarah's father, again out of breath, gasped, "What's going on?" as he just joined them next to his front door.

"Mr. Fields," the female officer answered calmly as her partner still passed, muttering to himself. We are responding to an emergency call at your home when we meet Mr. Daxter here. He is the one who made the call, " the female officer said authoritatively, nodding toward Jack.

"Sarah?" Mr. Fields called.

"Is Sarah all right? What happened?" He called, looking around for her, almost breaking past Jack and the officer for the front door.

"I'm here," Sarah said from behind the male angry officer.

Sarah's dad moved to hug her but was cut short by the disgruntled officer. "Yes, she is here," he said, taking hold of her arm, keeping her from her father.

"It seems little Miss Hermione Granger here called her love-sick Ron Weasley puppet fool to get some attention and gave him an excuse to feel like a hero when he probably couldn't replace a lightbulb without an instructional video. So, he decides to call us and tells us that an assailant was in your home with your daughter when he should be studying, doing community service, practicing flipping hamburgers, testing bulletproof vests, being a crash dummy, and making balloon animal snakes, and earthworms because that's all he is going to be good…"

"Hey, go check the perimeter." The female officer sighed. After they exchanged looks, she added, "That's an order!"

Standing firm, offering an angry look of pleading to his superior officer, he turned and looked at everyone before staring Jack down, grinding his teeth.

"What?" Jack had taken about enough of what he could from him. "Are you treating me like this because you're jealous? I don't have to carry my collection of replaced CDs, cassette tapes, and A-tracks like you for your squad car. Try Spotify, ya fossil."

"Oh, that's it," the officer called, pulling for his tazer. "Prepare to lose all bodily functions in front of the only girl you've seen from the right side of the screen."

"Enough" Get back, Officer Shirly, before I report you again.

Officer Shirly's expression turned from anger to sadness. He slumped away, his shoulders fallen, muttering to himself.

They watched him leave before the sound officer continued, "Everything is all right, Mr. Fields." She pulled Sarah forward so her father could hold her, and Jack could be beside them.

"I am going to let both of these youths off with a warning."

"A warning?!" Officer Shirly cried from afar.

"Yes, a warning," She bellowed back over her shoulder at him. "If you don't shut up, I'm going to move the coffee maker farther from your desk and put it next to the lady's bathroom, you germaphobe."

There was a gasp of horror before Officer Shirly dropped out of sight. All four who remained held a charged moment together as the female officer finished writing on a ticket pad. Jack kept glancing from the officer to Sarah's house. Mr. Fields tried to hold Sarah close while she gently tried moving away from her dad, not meeting his confused look. The female officer tore off the ticket and held it out for them to take.

"Have a good night, and please only call if it's an emergency." She said once Mr. Fields took it.

"Shirly?" Jack gasped as the female officer passed him. "His name is Shirly.... Perfect."

"That's it?" Shirly pleaded in disbelief from nowhere. "You're not going to do anything else? That kid is just trying to look like a hero when he only dialed three numbers on his phone and hit a green button. He is using us!"

"Hey," Jack called back. "Have a good time with your next cavity search for the world's hotdog eating contest finals winner."

Officer Shirly's head shot up from next to the car, "I'm going..." "Get in the car now!" the polite officer ordered. "The coffee is moving."

"What?" he hollered like a wounded hound. "Why does everything bad happen to me?" He cried, switching from anger to a pile of shame before they drove away.

"You! In the house!" Mr. Fields ordered Sarah. "You!" Turning on Jack, "Home and don't call tonight!"

"Mr. Fields! She called me and..."

"Enough!" He called, taking Sarah by the arm softly. "Go now, and she will not have her phone, so don't even try it." He pulled her up the front walkway. Sarah looked pleadingly at Jack as she was dragged away. He just stood there helpless as the door closed, separating them.

"I don't know what has gotten into you these past few days." Her dad thundered. "What is it?" He asked angrily, walking from the front room into the dining room and back again as if he didn't know where he was going.

"I was in the middle of a history seminar, and I was called offstage by Officer Lansing, and he tells me this to come home to this."

Sarah recognized that name. She knew Officer Lansing from their school. The weight of her dad's voice caused her to lower her head as she held her arms and crossed her legs.

"So, what is it?" He asked again. "Is it your friends? Is it your team? Is it drugs? Are you on drugs? The way some kids are acting, I hope they're on drugs, and that's why. Please don't look at me and say you were messing with that kid out there in the hopes that you'd get a sugar high on the sweets you want him to send you because you want him to like you." He waved, indicating the door where Jack had been left standing. "Is it movies? Or the strange music going around now? What is that group now, the Dead Ocean or something? Oh, speaking of sugar. I need it." Her dad rambled into the kitchen and opened cabinet after cabinet until he found a sugar doughnut.

He almost shoved the entire thing into his mouth, turning on Sarah, who hadn't moved. "Would peanut butter help?" she asked quietly.

Her dad choked. He blew pieces of powdered sugar and raspberry filling all over the kitchen. Coughing and gagging, hunched over the sink. Sticking his head under the faucet, he tried to clear his throat. Sarah stretched her neck higher to get a better view as it looked like he was suffering from hip tension and an anxiety attack combined.

Cough, cough. "What did you say?" her dad gasped, his head still in the sink, turning the water off.

Sarah suddenly found a strength inside her that she never knew was there. Her hands no longer shook as a warm feeling filled her chest. She raised her head and straightened her posture. "Peanut butter," she said more firmly. "I noticed we are missing some."

"Oh," her dad coughed, running a hand through his wet hair. "Yeah," he said as he looked around the kitchen. His eyes stopped on the cabinet where he had removed some of the food he had brought upstairs. Standing despairingly, he nervously straightened his tie, the end of which had fallen into the garbage disposal.

They stared at each other for what seemed like an hour. She looked back at him as he watched her, searching behind her eyes for something. The feeling of strength was leaving her as she almost laughed at the strange look on her father's face.

"AH!" her dad cried suddenly. Sarah screamed and leaped off the floor in shock. "I have to go!" he said with a burp pounding on his chest, still coughing.

"What?" Sarah asked in astonishment.

"The lecture! They are waiting for me to finish my lecture. The faculty and city council," he shrieked, turning in a circle. "I have to go to your room; you finish my speech. Give me my phone," he said, holding out a wet hand.

Sarah eyed him cautiously as he surged toward her. She took out her phone and handed it to him while he took out his keys with the other. He grabbed her forcibly and pulled her up the stairs.

"Go to your room and stay there. Don't come out, and when I get back, I expect you gone." He thundered, shutting her door. "Wait in the kitchen for me!"

"Dad, I haven't eaten." Sarah cried, reaching for her doorknob.

"Good, I'm not hungry either, " he coughed. Sarah stood perplexed as her dad shut her inside her room. The last thing he saw of her was her shocked, open mouth staring at her door. Her father's footsteps didn't lead down the stairs but toward his office. She leaned forward and placed her ear to her door. It sounded like a bull was trashing the room down the hall before the footsteps came crashing back toward her room.

"Stay in there!" He cried, hurrying down the hallway. "Don't come out before I get ho… ahh." The sounds of thud, bang, clunk, and yelps of pain told her that he was falling down the stairs. His scream grew even higher and climaxed with one cough when he hit the bottom. "I'm all right! I'm alllllright!" He called from below. "Just stay in your room. I'm locking you in! Uh, Love you." Slam! He shut the front door so hard that her room shook.

Sarah's eyes widened as she turned her home security app on her computer and saw her father limp to their car. He was in bad shape, his shirt untucked, covered in water, and holding his head. He backed up, crushing their bushes, and bent their mailbox. Their neighbors' lights turned on as they watched him slam on the gas, flying down the sidewalk and street.

Sarah bit her lip, wondering what had happened. She sat on the bed as it all rolled over again in her mind. She had never seen her dad act this way. What was the big secret?

"What is going on?" She instinctively reached into her pocket for her phone. Her shoulders fell as if she didn't feel anything there. In frustration, she fell backward on her bed.

Ding! She opened her eyes and looked over at her computer. The sound indicated that someone was trying to video chat her. She sprang from her bed and clicked on the link. It took so long to load before three faces appeared.

"You have no idea how badly I needed to see you guys," Sarah bellowed, almost yelling.

"What is going on? Are you all right?" Rachael asked.

"Jack told us that your life was better than a late-night talk show or The View, so what's the latest?" Shaw asked, shaking with excitement.

"We are so worried about you," Jack said, meaning Sarah and Shaw. They all spoke simultaneously and told the other how Jack had spoken to each of them. Thankfully, they didn't allow Sarah to talk until they all had finished. When they were done, Sarah struggled to find her voice. Sounding raspy, she told them how her father had told her to stay in her room and that he had left in shambles.

"Nice!" Shaw smirked, nodding shrewdly.

"Nice?" Rachael asked in derision. "He may be having a nervous breakdown. I heard of a teacher once who couldn't take the strain and became heterophobic and ran screaming out of his class. They found him a week later in the basement of Baskin Robins praying to a toilet paper roll, surrounded by Hawaiian paper umbrellas, wearing only a suit coat, tie, and a smile."

"What does being afraid of helicopters have to do with this?" Jack scorned.

"Whoop y'al, the point is, what are we going to do to help Sarah?" Shaw asked.

Sarah watched her friends' three confused faces as they stared back at her screen. She felt her strength rise once more, and she felt the thrill of freedom joining friendship. But she couldn't think of anything they could do.

"We must find out what is going on for her," Jack stated, sounding braver than he looked. "But I don't know how. My parents put me on lockdown after the police called them. What made it worse was that cop who didn't go to Disneyland enough as a kid who called them."

"Sneak out," Shaw said it with the same vaguer explaining to children how to clap.

"What?" Rachael and Jack said together.

"All you need is a butter knife, whipped cream, and a Jolly Rancher, and you must leave your phone. I'll talk you through it. How long is your dad-slave going to be gone?" Shaw asked.

"At least two hours," Sarah replied over Jack and Rachael's questioning of Shaw's list of escape needs.

"Oh-kay!" Shaw barked. "Meet at Sarah's in twenty. Jack, I will call you and walk you through the escape plan. Then I have to breathe in some of my Sulfur Hexafluoride to deepen my voice before I call your mom.

"Sulfur Hexafluoride! What?" Rachael and Jack tried to say.

"Wait, no! We can't! I can't!" Sarah objected. But before she could do anything else, they were gone. She stared, open mouth, at her computer screen, dumbfounded.

She jumped from her chair as if a light was suddenly turned on in her mind. She pointed at the screen and then at her door, biting her lower lip and growling in frustration. She grabbed her hands through her long, dark hair. She let it go, swinging her arms around in front of the door, then her closet, window, computer, television, sitting, hopping, over and over.

Ding-dong. Panicking, she looked at the clock on her wall, then her watch, ending with her computer. They all said at the same time. It was her friends; how could the time go by so fast? She reached for her doorknob and froze. She pictured her father ranting in anger. They had never had a problem like this before, nor had she openly gone against him. If she let go and stayed in her room, things would return to how they were. Her fingers loosened before she remembered all the questions she wanted answered. Without realizing it, she opened the door. She was shocked at what she was doing while she went down the stairs. It was like her body was making decisions for her.

"I can't-I don't believe this," Sarah exclaimed as she opened the door.

"What!? That a couple of friends come to your house for a lovely night of study and intellectual reflection?" Rachael said proudly, stepping in first.

"Sweeeeet! Your floors look so clean." Shaw said, smiling as he looked around.

"Are you all right?" Jack asked, stepping in quickly.

CHAPTER FOUR

I Got My Ears from My Grandma, Apparently.

"I don't know if I want to do this," Sarah complained, twirling her fingers. She shut the door and stood behind it, shaking.

"Are you all right?" Jack asked again in the same tone.

"Wow, your ceiling is as clean as your floor, not one footprint around the lights," Shaw said, sounding like a cartoon, "and no bugs."

"Sarah?"

"Yes, Jack, I'm okay!" Sarah spat back at him. "Things-things-" Sarah stuttered. "Things just aren't making sense to me right now."

"What are you talking about?" Rachael inquired, looking at Sarah's bookshelf in the hallway at the bottom of her stairs.

"Stuff with my dad, and well, you know, just, like drama," Sarah said, holding her forehead and running her other hand through her hair.

"Yeah, stuff," Shaw said absentmindedly, looking for spider webs in the corners.

"What drama?" Jack asked.

"Requiem!" Rachael exclaimed. "I have heard of that book," she said, taking it off the bookshelf. "I could relate to the main character, but…" She was not able to finish as there was that same clicking and sliding noise from upstairs that silenced them all. Each of their heads turned toward the noise and then to each other. Sarah hoped her eyes were not as comprehensive as her friend's as they shared this silent moment in shock.

"What was that?" Rachael asked.

"It was cool, that's what it was," Shaw called excitedly.

"I thought you said that your dad wasn't home?" Jack asked.

"Dude, why do you sound so scared?" Shaw enquired as he hopped toward the stairs.

"Rachael, put that book back!" Sarah ordered. "Shaw, stay put, and Jack, stop being so scared. My dad isn't home, so you can stop looking like you're going to wet your pants. My dad isn't even that good a shot."

"What do you mean, shot?" Jack sounded even more fearful.

"Shaw, get down. Rachael, stop him." Sarah said, following Shaw, who had started ascending the stairs.

Shaw kept going eagerly up the stairs, singing softly, "There's a lady who's sure all that glitters is gold, and she's buying a stairway to heaven. When she gets there, she knows…"

"Shaw, come down!" Sarah ordered, following him.

"Are we going up?" Rachael inquired. "I thought we were gathering for emotional strengthening. You know, some Les Brown talks, or even Nick Vujicic. I have the 7 Habits of Highly Effective People eBook on my phone. Can't we just read together or something? Hey, wait!"

"Don't leave me here." Jack whimpered, running after them suddenly.

Each clamored up the stairs in their way. Shaw acted like it was Christmas, looking for his present. Sarah yelled at him to get back downstairs wishing to contain her friends. Rachael rattled off sections from the book The Power of Positive Thinking while Jack clung to her, looking like a scared human backpack.

All the while, Shaw sings, "Your stairway lies on the whispering wind as we wind down the road. Our shadows are taller than our soul; there walks a lady we all-ah! Here it is." Shaw stopped singing and walked into the study belonging to Sarah's father.

"I am not even supposed to come in here; now, let's get downstairs," Sarah ordered again, following Shaw.

"Maybe he has test answers in here?" Shaw asked himself.

"Cheating is the last resort of the desperate," Rachael answered.

"Look at all the old stuff," Jack said, finally letting go of Rachael.

Shaw went to the desk on the far side of the room, covered in papers, before a large computer. Rachael admired the glass cases with ancient memorabilia stored and preserved in them.

"Wow, look at all the books!" Jack said breathlessly. He ran his hands over the walls lined with them, and more were stacked on the floor.

"It smells like my grandma's closet in here," Shaw whispered, waving the air away in front of his nose.

"Guys," Sarah said firmly. "I have had enough of this. Get out now."

"What's this?" Jack asked, pushing against some books on the bookshelf on the east wall softly. It moved in a little as if part of the wall was loose.

"Don't touch," Sarah called, but Jack had pushed harder before she could finish. A wall section moved in, revealing an unlit passage and some stairs leading up.

"That must have been the noise we heard downstairs," Rachael said smartly.

"Dope! Man, that's dope!" Shaw called, craning his head to get a better look. "What's up there?"

"I don't want to know." Sarah gulped.

"Is this the way to your attic?" Jack asked, craning his neck from the left side of the door to look up.

"No," Sarah answered. "It's down the hallway. Now, please, can we all go? My dad will come home, and I don't want to know what is up there or what is going on."

"Shaw, wait!" Rachael said. Shaw had already taken a step to go up the stairs. Her voice was calm and controlled, unlike Sarah's scared and panicking tone, but Shaw stopped when he heard it.

"A secret passage in your home?" Jack said. "That's lit, but I'm here if your dad comes home. O.M. Goat-ness. He is going to milk me like a goat."

"Don't you want to know what's up there?" Rachael asked coolly. "You have had a difficult past few days, and the questions you cannot bear are consuming you. The answers you seek must be up those steps. Why are you feeling fear and weakness? Shaw, help me out here."

"Honestly, I got to tell you. I'm still trying to figure out why a goat?" Shaw said normally. "Who milks a goat? What is this 'Little House on the Prairie' all of a sudden? Come on, Jack, climb that beanstalk." Shaw waved up the stairs. "The cow is still fertile for milking. You don't have to sell her for magic beans or milk the goat."

"Thanks for the help," Rachael said, eyeing him stupidly.

"You're welcome." He responded as if he had.

Jack's bloodless, white face changed when he looked at Sarah. His eyes seemed to be filling with sentiment. "Look, I want to get out of here before your dad makes me feel like a creeper every time I'm at school. But I think you should find the answers to what's bothering you."

"If I just peek up those stairs, can we go then, please?" Sarah asked, taking a step forward.

"Yeah. Yeah. No." Jack and Rachael replied positively, but Shaw was negative. They all turned to look up the stairs as Sarah took tiny steps forward. It was as if she had been called into the principal's office. The stairs were surprisingly clean from dust and didn't even squeak. With each step, she took a deep breath. She was almost halfway when she stopped. She turned to see that her friends had formed a human centipede, walking closely packed behind her. All three of them had a different expression on their face. Shaw was excited and smooth. Rachael was indifferent, and Jack was terrified.

"Uh, I will be all right. You don't have to come." Sarah whispered.

"We know." All three said as if they were planning to say it together. After all, it was her home, and all she was doing was going upstairs in her home. Just a strange, mysterious, hidden, secluded staircase in her home that her father had kept secret from her.

Sarah shook her head and took another step up the stairs, then another. A soft light came from somewhere down the far side of a room at the top of the stairs. It was reflecting on the attic ceiling, pointed and lined with rafters. She thought that they looked like the ribs of her house. Little dots on the insulation between them glimmered like star constellations. Higher and higher she went, seeing more and more. It looked like someone had mapped out the entire sky on a clear night on the ceiling.

She had come up one end of the room and could see across the room from her. The walls seemed to drop as she rose. They were covered in untidy papers strung all over—layer after layer of information, writings, hand-drawn maps, and newspaper clippings. A circular wood table with elegant chairs stood in the center of the large room. The light in the room came from a television, and in front of it was a large, comfortable couch. On it was a single person watching with their back to Sarah.

She kept going, not knowing why now, as curiosity had stopped her thinking. She reached the top of the stairs to see the floor was covered with a thick shag red carpet. A fridge, dresser, and the most wonderful bed she had ever seen was in the room. Against the wall were all kinds of small animal traps. There must have been a hundred of them. She walked toward the table and was amazed at its handwork and scroll carvings. Behind her was a computer with the largest mainframe she had ever seen and, more surprisingly, museum-type items. Everything from a suit of armor, swords, saddles, crossbows, ballroom outfits, piles and piles.

She walked by the table, mesmerized by the person sitting on the couch. It was the head of an old, white-haired man watching an old I Love Lucy episode. The light from the television and the strange, magical-like stars guided her steps. She crept on until she was almost next to the sofa.

The older man had pale white skin and robust features. His ears were abnormally large, hairy, and pointed on top. The television illuminated his snowy face, deepening the shadows in his eyes and the aged lines in his face. His focus was fixed on the black-and-white screen as it changed to an episode of The Munsters. Sarah made no noise as she cautiously kept moving to see more of the man's face. The man wore an attractive red housecoat that rose to his neck. His head slowly turned towards her. His yellow eyes were like two candles giving light of their own. His ancient face seemed cracked apart by a smile showing two sharp fangs.

"Sarah, you bear your grandmother's resemblance of youth." The ancient albino-like man said warmly.

"AAAAHHHHHH!" came four crescendoing screams as they ran toward the stairway and hidden door. Sarah was so focused on the man in front of the television that she hadn't noticed her friends having followed close behind her.

Rachael and Jack jumped over Shaw, who had fallen. Sarah unconsciously jumped over him, leaping down the stairs. She stumbled and fell to the floor of the study while still screaming. Jack and Rachael pushed the bookshelf closed and braced themselves against it.

"It won't stay shut!" Jack yelled. *Wham!* Something smashed hard against the door, almost causing Rachel and Jack to fall over. They forced the door back as books fell about them. Screams came from both sides of the doorway. *Bang! Bang! Bang!* The door was hit again and again as Rachel and Jack pushed back against it.

"The book!" Rachael shouted. "The book downstairs needs to be put back to lock the door." She put her shoulder against the door and pushed back hard. "Sarah, go!"

Sarah rose, favoring her left ankle, feeling she must have twisted it when she landed. She almost reached the door when Rachael's cell phone started ringing.

"Don't answer it!" Sarah thundered, leaning on the door frame.

"No, I'm calling for help," Rachael answered, putting her back to the trap door.

As soon as Rachel hit Answer, there was an ear-splitting yell from its speaker. "OPEN THE FRIKEN DOOR!" Shaw yelled.

"Oh…" Jack whimpered, taking a step back. Rachael didn't move as quickly and was thrown to the floor as Shaw erupted from the hidden room. His face was as white as the older man they had seen. He only let out a small mouse-like squeak before he flew from the office. Jack and Rachael were right behind him. Rachael called out apologies, and Jack bellowed questions at him.

"Wait, don't leave me here with it!" Sarah cried as she tried to follow them. Shaw, Rachael, and Jack barely touched the floor as they flew down the stairs toward the front door.

"Wait, wait! Please wait!" Sarah yelled, hobbling down the stairs. As Rachael passed the bookshelf, she pushed back the key book. From the office came the clicks and sliding noise sealing the trap door. The front door burst open, leaving Sarah leaning heavily on the stair railing. The others ran out screaming bloody murder, leaving her to look on. When they left her view, they were replaced with the figure of her father standing alone, watching in bewilderment five steps away from the front door. All Sarah could do was quietly limp to the front door and search for her friends before she just shut the door.

CHAPTER FIVE

HISTORY IS CRYSTAL CLEAR

"Sarah, what is going on?" her dad asked once he came home. As soon as he came in, she saw him looking utterly confused, holding his briefcase in one hand and wiping his forehead with a handkerchief in the other.

"Well, chair, wheal, snow, pain, hamster, orbofibans," She muttered oddly, turning from the bookshelf to her room, the office, and back to her father.

"Enough!" He yelled. He didn't sound angry, just loud as he shut the door behind him. "I gave my speech and excused myself to come home to *this*? What is going on?"

"I, uh," Sarah groaned. "I asked you first."

"What?" he asked, letting his briefcase go. "You know, never mind!" His tone changed from anger to hysteria. "I don't want to know! I want to go to bed and wash my mouth with two hundred Tylenol. You will go to bed and not speak to those friends who ran out of here as if they had just robbed the place."

"Dad, I, I," Sarah said, still mumbling.

"Please, no more words."

"But, Dad?"

"Sarah, Please!" He yelled, taking a step forward.

"David." A cold voice came from the top of the stairs.

Sarah spun around to see the old man from the hidden room standing at the top of the stairs. In his old, white, twisted hand, he held something that shone a soft green color.

"What are you doing?" Her dad asked him, panicking. "Get to the room."

"She needs to know!" The old man stated confidently.

"We have been over this," her dad cried hysterically. "She doesn't need to know. She can't know. The line is broken, and there is nothing that we can do about it. The end is coming, and I want her to live her days out happily. I want to be with her and enjoy the time we have left."

"David, look," the old man said, holding the greenish object in his hands.

"It, it can't be." Her dad said, looking shocked. "How?"

Both their eyes moved to look at Sarah, who was frozen in fear. Suddenly, things started to seem blurry and dark. The last thing she remembered was the fuzzy figure of her dad lunging at her as she started to faint.

"Sarah," someone asked from far away. "Sarah, wake up." It sounded again, this time sounding closer.

She opened her sticky eyes and strived to have her eyes focus on something. Blinking seemed to help as she gathered a blurry outline above her, which was her father's face. The way her back felt also told her she was lying on something soft. Unconsciously smiling from those two feelings also made her realize everything else was dark and that she didn't know where she was. Then, there was a new sound left of her. Turning her head to see what it was

"Whoooaa," she yelled, sitting up quickly and spinning around to cower in the couch corner.

"What's that crazy used twisted tissue doing here?" She screamed as her father restrained her.

"Sarah, relax. Everything is all right," he ordered. We will tell you everything. Just sit down."

"What is that thing? He looks like he went to the first ever Comicon in the 1800s, and Rip Van Winkled in our attic?" She rapidly slapped her father's hands away and frantically felt her neck for puncture marks.

"You brought me up to the attic to suck me as dry as Trump's hair." Finding nothing on her neck, she thrust out her arms and crossed her fingers, forming a plus sign.

"Sarah, calm down," her father urged, letting go of her as she backed away. The elderly white man seemed hurt by her words and cowered back.

"Calm down?" Sarah coughed. "Okay, all right. I will calm down. What is *he* for? Our night watchman? Or is he a Twilight disco ball in the sunlight? You tell me."

"Don't get hysterical." The old man consoled softly.

She had climbed over the couch and backed up more and more, not knowing where she was going, and kept her crossed fingers up. Her hip hit the round table, and her father and the older man moved toward her, standing side by side.

"Sarah, just sit down, and we will tell you everything." Her dad said, urging her to relax. The older man nodded quickly in agreement.

"Oh, I will do that as soon as the garlic pizza I order arrives." She said, making her way around the table. "I want to know how you floss, brush or do any personal hygiene when you don't have a reflection in the mirror."

"Sarah, watch out!" Her dad cried and lunged forward.

Her eyes had not left the two men, and she did not notice the stairs behind her. She lost her footing and started falling backward down the stairway toward the hidden door. She braced herself for the hard landing she was expecting to have when *whoosh*! Something caught her.

Stunned, as the walls and everything had stopped. She looked to see what had stopped her and found that the older man had abruptly crossed the room in the blink of an eye and caught her. Shaken, she looked into his face.

"I won't let anything happen to you," he said kindly, helping her to her feet.

"Ahhhh!" She screamed again, leaping from his arms, and ran to the other side of the room to her father. He wrapped her up in the biggest hug she had had since she could remember. It seemed to go on for hours before she started to let him go. Remembering there was an old vampire in the room, she grabbed her dad again and jerked her head over to watch him. The old man hadn't moved from where he had caught her. His warm smile was also unchanged.

"Sarah, you need to try to calm down, " her dad said, leading her back to the couch.

"Just try and relax. We have debated on telling you this for so long."

"Tell me what?" Sarah asked resignedly.

"Your history," her dad said, looking her in the eye. "Our history," he said, looking up at their pale companion still standing back by the stairs.

Sarah's dad removed his glasses and cleaned them with his tie. Coughing slightly, he thoughtfully stuck his tongue to the side of his mouth. Once he got a reassuring nod from the older man, he put his glasses back on and started.

"This goes back to the year 1066 when some people saw a comet in the sky. It was larger than the glow of Venus, and they took it as an omen. The people then took the comet as a sign of victory in battle. Anglo-Saxon King Harold the Second was at war with Duke William the Second of Normandy. The history books say they were fighting for England, but they weren't. The conquerors share those stories."

Her father stopped lecturing as if he were in his class and sat beside her. He seemed more excited now, as if telling her this relieved a great pain he had carried for a long time. "Centuries later, the evil that threw England into war started to rise again. In the 15th century, a man left for Transylvania on business. It was a huge deal for him. Before he left, he kissed his wife and three children goodbye, as this trip would change all their lives. They were poor and needed the money; he wanted the best life for them. He was given the strictest instructions he followed because he only thought of their welfare. He didn't even listen to the people in Transylvania who tried to warn him. The deal would provide clothes for his children, jewelry for his wife, and a better home. He was centered on getting them the life they deserved."

"Don't stray too far from the story." The older man said from behind them.

His voice made Sarah jump a little. She had forgotten all about him, and that scared her. How could she forget about HIM? Before she could give it another thought, her father continued.

"This man went on to Borgo Pass and gave the lease to an Abbey in London and all the travel documents to a very extraordinary client. His work was done, and, in his heart, he was the happiest of men because he had secured what his family needed for the future. Then everything changed."

"What?" Sarah asked expectantly.

"A vampire bit him." The old man said. Her father's eyes fell to the floor.

Time stopped. Sarah didn't even blink. "Wwwwaaaaiiittt!" She said, almost laughing.

"It's true!" Her dad cried pleadingly. "I swear it!"

Sarah watched him through the corner of her eyes as a smile started to cross her face.

"It was Dracula," her dad continued, not giving her a chance to say or do anything new. He was talking more quickly now as he got to his feet. He paced back and forth in front of her, now relaying the story.

"He had brought this man with him on board the schooner Vesta back to England. The crew and captain were thought to be killed in the storm and almost lost the ship at sea. He was the sole survivor but was diagnosed as a lunatic. They thought he was driven mad in the storm and was put under the watchful eye of Dr. John Seward, who treated him. We have copies of his records and notes here somewhere. This man wasn't mad like any other; he was hypnotized and being controlled by Dracula. Count Dracula promised him anything, everything if he would but obey him. But this man, through all that, fought the dark hold on him because the memory of his family was still there in the back of his mind. He fought back against his master, and for his rebellion, he was thrown down the stone steps of Carfax Abbey."

"Dracula killed him?" Sarah asked in mocking shock, raising her hand to her chest.

"This is not something to laugh about!" Her dad argued. He sat back down next to her.

"Ok, sorry to break the mood here." Clearing her throat. Her dad gave her a look that told her to get rid of her raised eyebrows and smile.

Standing back up, he went on. "You don't stop a vampire by throwing him down the stairs." Her dad was rubbing his forehead again like he had when he had to concentrate. "That night, Dracula was killed by Dr. Van Helsing. They were the ones who found this man. He was bruised and had his crushed back, bones, and neck broken but he was still alive. They took him and cared for him."

"Wait! That wasn't in the movie." Sarah yelled in confusion.

"Good, you remember," the old man in the back said excitedly.

"The doctors who treated him didn't tell others everything. Those secrets they kept for a select few. Those few who would take on the cause against darkness. The family of those who fought before and do to this day. The Odyssey Knights!"

"Right," Sarah said flatly.

"She doesn't believe me." Her dad said, turning to lean on the television.

"Sarah," the old man said behind her. She turned slowly to take in his whole frame. "The man who your father was talking about was R.M. Renfield. I changed my last name after the accident to Field, and I am your grandfather.

"The man I was talking about is right there, " her dad said, pointing to her grandfather. Sarah didn't say anything but felt her jaw drop.

"Dracula wasn't and can't be killed," her dad said, not looking at her but staring off into nothingness. "He can only be delayed."

"Evil cannot be killed, but it can be deflected." Her grandfather continued, taking a step forward.

"Dracula came to England not just for new blood, freedom with new ignorance but also to claim something from under that Abbey. It was a small crystal shard. No one knew of it but your grandfather, and by the time he regained his ability to talk, only Dr. Van Helsing and Seward believed him."

"What was he doing?" Sarah said, now interested.

"Vampires cannot live in sunlight." Her father stated. "The first war that was told to be between The Duke of Normandy and The Saxon King was actually between them and the armies of Darkness. Dracula ruled over all that fear the light, sirens, cyclops, ogres, demons, zombies, chimeras, centaurs, banshees, shads, basilisks, goblins, pixies, hobgoblins, imps, and werewolves, to name a few. Dracula was about to perform a ritual, a terrible ritual, but the Duke and King stopped him. Your grandfather learned that he was going to try again."

"Try what?" Sarah asked. She was intrigued despite herself.

"Every few hundred years, a comet comes close to Earth. Centuries ago, a piece of it fell and was unknown to humankind until Saint Thomas found it and knew what it was. He brought it back to Rome, where it was guarded year after year. We don't know how he did it, but one day, it was gone. Dracula somehow learned of it and had it brought to him. When the comet was close to Earth, his plan was to get that piece back into space. The light from the sun would shine through it and down on his army, freeing them from their weakness to sunlight forever. The armies of darkness would control this world in a matter of days. Your grandfather convinced his caretakers to bring him to the Vatican. They gathered the Knights and followed Dracula back to Transylvania. Dracula was ready for them."

"Dad," Sarah said hesitantly. "I don't know how much more I can listen about this."

"I know."

"She must," the old man insisted from behind them.

"You can't expect to tell her everything and have her accept it in a matter of minutes," her dad shot back.

"She must! We are running out of time." Sarah kept looking between them as if it were a verbal tennis match.

"What if I prove it to her?" Her grandfather asked quietly.

"NO!" Sarah shouted. "You keep those bottle-opening fangs to yourself!"

"Just look at me for a moment if you please," he said, sounding stronger. "I won't do anything to you. I am going to alter my appearance slightly."

"You are going to change your clothes in front of me?" Sarah asked in disgust. "I know you just said we are family, but we are never going to be *that* close of a family."

"Just watch," both her father and grandfather said simultaneously.

She instinctively closed her eyes but thought, what could they do to her? If they wanted to hurt her, they would have done it already. They did warn her. One eye opened and then the other.

A rye smile appeared on the older man's face. "All right, what to do, what to do?" he asked, rubbing his chin. "Oh, I got it." He closed his eyes as Sarah watched him stand there doing nothing. Suddenly, the wrinkles on his face started to fade as his skin tightened. His white hair began to darken. His posture straightened, and he appeared to look younger than her father in seconds.

"How's this?" he asked, sounding young and vibrant.

"Dad, you're a ghoul!" Her father said, almost laughing.

"What?! This is how I looked back then," her grandfather said, running his fingers through his hair and flexing his muscles.

"How'd you do that?" Sarah asked in shock.

"First, let your father finish," the younger version of her grandfather said. Taking a bow, he waved to her father and said, "Carry on David."

"Before they left, the Pope blessed a tool to fight Dracula. It was more of a weapon then a tool come to think of it. It is called the Telum Deos amulet. If needed, it would bless the wearer with increased strength, speed, shield, and a weapon when called upon. I forgot the particulars, but It could only be worn by one of the sacred bloodlines of the first who bore it into battle. You know, for the next part, maybe it would be better for your Grandfather to show you." Her father waved to her younger version grandfather, wanting him to sit beside her as he stepped back.

Before she knew it, her younger-looking grandfather appeared beside her with an excited look all over him. "Wait, what are you going to do to me?" She cried, leaning away from him.

"Don't worry, my dear," her grandfather said, looking kind. "I will never do anything that would harm your person, ever."

His smile seemed to warm her as she felt a sudden pull to look into his eyes. She reached up, moved her long blond hair away from her eyes, and found her neck, turning her head toward him. Their eyes met like her heartbeat enhanced to feel the beating of a drum in her chest. In her mind, her thoughts were pulled like a rubber band. She felt warm and relaxed as everything before her was pulled away.

"We had gathered together in a village below Dracula's Castle. The knights, priests, and community leaders had gathered to discuss how to attack." Her grandfather's voice said in her mind. It was as if she saw that time in a gray haze of his memory playing like a movie in her mind.

"We must attack at first light when they are weak!" The man shouting didn't identify himself, but somehow Sarah knew it was the village's mayor.

"Nao," said a strong woman's voice. She was once a schoolteacher but had been a victim of an attack, which the community didn't believe until recently. *"Eef we wait ahnd ze*

rumahrs ahre true we will ahll die, or wahrse. I do naht eentend to give heem ze oppahrtuneety to be hees ahgain. we must ahct ahs soon ahs we cahn."

"*Maltese,*" Granao cried, pounding the table they sat and stood around. He was the best blacksmith in the area. A large, bearded man who had one child lost three years ago. "*We cannot just charge up unknowing.*"

"*Ahnd whaht eef we do wait?*" Maltese shouted back louder than he did. She leaned over the table, glaring at him. "*Whaht ahre we waiteeng to find out, how to be food, a cheeld's play things, hees meestress. Oh yes, I would lahve to see zem mahke you dress up een my red lahce treemmed skeempy skeert. you slow peeg.*"

She slapped her hand on the table hard just as he had done, "*We must ahct!*"

"*We must act, yes,*" Bishop Paul said. He waved his hands up and down, encouraging them to calm down. "*But we must not act rashly or amongst ourselves. Colossians 3:15, Let the peace of Christ rule in your hearts since as members of one body you were called to peace.*"

All twelve who were present bowed their heads and made the sign of the cross on their chest. They shared a moment of silence, glancing at one another.

"*If the rumors are true,*" said the innkeeper where they met. "*We may not have the time we want. The sign comes tonight, and if he…*" He paused for a moment. "*If they succeed, we may not have another day.*"

"*Ahnd whaht eef we lahse, ah? We wahnt hahve ahnahthair chahnce aht ziss.*"

"*We have to find another way.*" A younger version of her grandfather said, coming into the light of the table. Sarah was surprised to see in her mind that he was wearing the clothes of a nobleman, a black tie, and a traveler's suit. *"Mr. Bran, you have been here the longest. You have been very quiet."*

Everyone turned to a single person outside the group gathered at the table to a lone older man in the corner of the Inn. He sat with a tall glass in front of him, half drunk. His weary old hand lifted it and drank enough of its contents to wet his lips. *"I was thinking about what to say when asked because I knew one of you would ask me. Your choice is to assault his Castle with almost everyone you have. You must do it before more of his army enters the forest to protect him."*

"You want us to charge into those thousands?" The blacksmith shouted in protest. *"In the hopes that we make it through to face whatever he has in the castle? Overcome them and then him?"*

"No, not all of you," Mr. Bran said quietly. Everyone held their breath to hear. *"A group must sneak in undetected in daylight and be with them just as night begins."*

"What!?" A few cried out and started to argue amongst themselves. The blacksmith pushed others aside and stepped forward toward the older man. *"How can we do that? Who is going to do it? Do you expect me…"*

"Do it," Mr. Bran said calmly. *"Or die."* Without another word, he flipped a coin onto his table to pay for his drink, rose, and shuffled out into the late afternoon street.

"He's right." The mayor said, more to himself. *"Wait! Boozbee go to the city archives and find a schematic of the grounds, plans, anything about his castle."* A small, mousy man ran from the table. The image went dark again in Sarah's mind.

"We found that in the Castle grounds, several passageways were implemented in its structure." Her grandfather's voice, Renfield, said in her mind. *"Thousands fought outside in the woods, buying time for us to enter the castle* undetected." She saw and heard a battle stretching for miles in the woods surrounding an

immense castle set on a hillside with the sun setting behind it. The clash of weapons, howls of pain, and victory were all below. The image returned as she saw Renfield and six others making their way cautiously up a stone passage under the castle, torches in hand guiding them on.

Their progress came to a halt before a large stone obstructed their way. Try as they might, no one could move it until Renfield stepped forward. He was able to move the heavy stone easily. It rolled out of the way, presenting the back of an elaborate tapestry hanging in a giant castle room. The great hall was not dusty nor showed signs of neglect. On the contrary, everything in the room stood immaculately well-kept, dusted, shined, and polished. Sarah saw Renfield's team fan out, moving quickly and quietly. They causally made their way toward the castle's center, working hard to avoid detection and bypassing evil sentries. A gorgon and a group of hobgoblins almost caught them if it wasn't for one of them sneezing on the others, causing a distracting fight. When suddenly, from around a corner, they were found by a group of myrmidons and scorpion men.

Sarah screamed in fear, forgetting she was a spectator and not presently there. She watched as three peeled from the group and engaged the enemy. The others ran on toward their goal while the rest fought on. A group of skeletons tried to cut them off. Sarah's eyes widened as she saw a double-bladed axe of light appear in Renfield's hands. He cut through them with astonishing speed. They fought on, the group splitting apart, each separating, trying to find Dracula.

The image hurried for a moment, like someone had hit the fast-forward button, to one of the large courtyards in the middle of the castle. It was a wide field two hundred yards in each direction. In the center was a large green glowing crystal the size of a grown man. Everything in Sarah's vision was darkened and hazy, save for the crystal. Renfield hid alone in bushes, searching the area surrounded by scattered, unfamiliar equipment. The crystal was suspended in the air by four thick cords tied off to the top of four high battlement pillars at each yard corner. There were creatures of every kind working, checking, and writing all around the courtyard. The bustle of activity stopped without a word as the hundreds of workers watched the sun's last light go down. They dropped to their knees, and an ear-splitting shriek was heard.

"He has awakened." Sarah heard her grandfather say in her mind.

Renfield moved lightning fast, faster than she had ever seen anyone move, to another secluded spot to see better.

"My Children!" A male voice called.

Sarah saw everyone's attention turn to a man walk into the courtyard. She was surprised to see that he didn't look at all evil. As a matter of fact, he was one of the most handsome men she had ever seen. There was power, charisma, and confidence about him. Every dark, disgusting creature bowed lower as he passed. And, just as Sarah knew the mayor when she saw him without being told, she knew that this was Dracula.

Dracula walked powerfully until he reached the crystal, then raised a hand and touched it as if caressing a loved one's face.

"My children," Dracula said again, nodding. *"We have been shunned by all those who call us evil."* He turned and watched his followers rise. *"Those who hunt us, kill us, call us sinful will finally pay for their murders."* There were shouts and calls of approval from all around them.

"Those who enjoy the light," Dracula continued his speech walking around the crystal. *"Those who glutton themselves, who do not know starvation, deprivation, will pay for their easy living. For once, we will take what they take for granted. We did not ask*

to be shunned or made the way we are. They judge us and slaughter us for no other reason than who we are. But tonight, this night, it will not have to be that way anymore. Tonight, we change the night into day. Tonight is our first day and their last night."

The cries and yells from his followers were so loud that even Renfield started to shrink, covering his ears; Sarah did the same. As they stopped, Dracula pointed to the sky and said, "*Behold, my children. Our salvation comes.*"

The vision turned toward the sky, and Sarah saw a comet soaring overhead. "*The time approaches. Prepare yourselves. Your future calls.*"

It looked as if the ground moved as every creature hastened to a position about the courtyard. "*Boozbee, are we ready?*"

"*Yes, master,*" came his sniveling voice. Sarah watched as the same man from the town meeting came out of the shadows toward Dracula.

"*The timing must be perfect,*" Boozbee said with a smile.

Something small tapped Renfield's back. He turned suddenly to see three of his fellow compatriots hiding not too far away. Sarah recognized Maltese, the blacksmith, and another leader from a nearby village. Maltese silently moved her lips and said the word "*Traitor.*"

"*Make ready!*" Dracula said with a smile.

"*Alarm master!*" came a call. It repeated over and over again. All heads turned toward something coming into the courtyard that Sarah couldn't see. Finally, a skeleton deprived of its lower half, was visible through a break in the bushes and equipment. It crawled its way toward Dracula on its hands, dragging its torso.

"*They have broken in,*" Dracula called. "*Defend the crystal. None must…*" The hastening of creatures slowed. A low laugh grew, bringing everyone to a halt again, and every eye was back on Dracula once more as his laughter grew and grew.

"They are already here!" He declared.

There were cries of war from both sides as Renfield's three followers sprang from their hiding places and charged. Hundreds of dark creatures came right at them. Dracula raised a hand and brought everything to a stop once again. The three from the village were frozen and stood unmoving by some magical force. Every evil creature stopped in fear.

"Let us not be so quick, my children," Dracula said with a smile. He went forward and looked at each of the three invaders in the eye, smiling wider at each one. *"Let us not kill them right away. After all, they did come all this way to do something. We would be inhospitable to ask them to leave so soon after they arrived. But my new friends, you do come uninvited."* Every dark creature laughed softly.

"The time has come for the chosen to pay tribute. Come forward."

Sarah watched Renfield pull deeper into the bush he was hiding in. He was about to spring out when he saw the pleading look of Maltese pleading him to wait. Dracula practically floated to the crystal and admired it like a newborn child. He raised his left-hand pointer fingernail and cut the palm of his right. Dark, black blood appeared, dripping down his wrist. Sarah noticed his fingers shaking with excitement as he placed his cut palm in the crystal.

Where his hand touched, the crystal's color changed. It was as if the crystal was filled with green water, and Dracula's blood were drops of dark dye. The dark dye swirled before the crystal grew brighter for a moment and began to pulsate. A member of each dark race came behind Dracula and repeated the process of offering their blood. The crystal repeated the same effect with each of them, glowing brighter until it shone more luminous than the torches in the courtyard.

Once completed, Dracula cried, *"Tis time!"* He was no longer fanciful but seemed more animal than man. *"Bring them!"* He waved a hand, and all three of Renfield's companions were pushed to the ground and immediately seized upon. Struggling, they were pulled to the crystal.

"Let us see what happens to you," Dracula said, smiling, taking Maltese's hand. She struggled but had absolutely no effect on his strength, as he cut her palm and forced her to place her hand on the crystal. The crystal's pulsing stopped for a moment and then reversed. Renfield readied himself, preparing to spring out of the bush.

"We have five minutes to go, master," Boozbee said from the side of the courtyard.

"Give the others' blood to the crystal," Dracula ordered, moving toward Boozbee.

"Wait!" Dracula cried again. Everyone froze as Dracula turned toward Renfield's hiding place. *"There is another!"*

Renfield sprung out of hiding, and a bow and arrow made of brilliant light appeared in his hands. Renfield fired a shot at the closest dark creature. The giant rat squeaked in pain and fell to the ground. Renfield kept shooting, cutting down everything that was coming at him. His bow changed back to light in his hands, then transformed into a gleaming double axe when there were too many for him at close range. He looked like he was cutting down tall, dark trees by the hundreds. Even they began to be too much for him. They suddenly overpowered him by sheer number and piled on him. Sarah gasped as Renfield was covered in darkness.

"One minute now, master," Boozbee yelled, standing in a far corner of the courtyard with one hand beside a long lever, the other holding a large watch. Dracula held out his hands in admiration of the crystal. Unexpectedly from the side Sarah

saw, Renfield leaped out of the dark mob. He rose ten feet into the air, and the light bow reappeared manifested in his hands. He aimed a shot at Dracula. Dracula's face only turned to him and smiled.

"Now!" Dracula cried to Boozbee. Boozbee quivering wet lips dripping with liquid courage, let out a scream of delight. He pulled down on the leaver, which resisted his force for a second before it gave freely. In between a heartbeat, Renfield started to come down from his jump and changed his aim to Dracula's side. He let loose a light arrow, not at Dracula but at the crystal. It flew and hit the lower part, breaking a shard off.

When the lever was flipped, the ropes holding the crystal started to tighten, and the towers holding them began to groan. Each of the four towers' battlements began to lean away from the courtyard, forcing the crystal to rise. Renfield landed in a heap of angry creatures while his three comrades fell as if released from Dracula's vile marionette strings. The ropes on the crystal tightened, and as the towers fell, the crystal was launched upward. Every eye watched it rise as the towers fell until the force of the towers' falling caused it to be released and fly into the sky.

"You're too late," Dracula called, spinning in a circle on him. Every eye watched; the battle stopped outside to see the crystal continue to climb into the sky. It grew smaller as it went on a straight line to meet the comet.

"Soon, they will collide!" Dracula said excitedly. *"When they do, the crystal will shatter and surround the earth. The sun's light will connect with them, covering the earth in evil and shrouding it in eternal darkness. We will never suffer from your light again!"*

Every dark creature howled triumphantly as the four heroes were held down into submission. The crystal became a tiny dot as the last stones of the towers stopped tumbling. Even the wind seemed to quiet as everything looked up.

"Boozbee, are you certain?" Dracula asked impatiently.

"Yes, master, I have done all you have asked. I have checked the facts over and over again. Now, will you give me what you promised?"

"Once all is done and not before," Dracula said, moving irritably.

Sarah saw Renfield being brought forward by four large cyclopes, each holding a limb. She thought he looked like a small piece of candy being fought over.

"Any moment now," Dracula said hungrily. *"It will be the dawn of a new day. A day of darkness!"*

But as they watched the comet come closer, it came right over them and kept going. Sarah thought that something miraculous should have happened, but nothing did.

Every creature slowly began moving uneasily, looking up and then to their master. The time they had been waiting for surely passed. The sounds of war and battle outside began again and were growing louder. The comet certainly must have passed its mark. Some of the creatures on the outskirts of the mob began to flee.

Dracula suddenly reared on Boozbee. *"You have failed me!"*

"No, master, I didn't! I didn't!" He screamed.

Then, the image went dark. Every dramatic feeling Sarah felt slowly gave way to peace, as if she were waking from a pleasant dream. Reality returned and she was now looking into her grandfather's eyes. He was no longer young but back to the form she had first seen him in. The sight frightened her.

Chapter Six

Time to Wash Your Mouth Out with a Reality Check

In seeing Sarah recoil a little, Renfield moved back slowly.

"I do apologize," he said. "Sometimes the demands of emotion tax the receiver to bring the memories to your mind."

"What was that?" Sarah gasped.

"Those proprietary thoughts were my memories of the past. It is what happened the day Dracula failed."

"But what happened after?" she asked looking at her father.

Both her father and grandfather shared a worried expression. Neither spoke a word, but their faces said they were concerned and concealing something. Sarah watched soberly until her grandfather answered. "Many lifetime's worth of events. The things of nightmares and dreams, the battle of good and evil waged on, but that night, we were spared, and evil was delayed."

"How did you get away? What happened to the three others and Dracula? What did happen…"

"All in good time, Sarah," her dad interrupted. "For the moment, focus on the most important thing, the Amulet. The Telum Deos. Life has come to it once more, and we might be able to fight again."

"That thing that lit up like my cell phone light? What about it?"

"Sarah," her grandfather said lovingly. "The Telum Deos is the one weapon we have against evil. It is the ultimate weapon. I wielded it as long as I could. Then your father did so until he couldn't. Now, we hope you may be able to use its power for humanity."

"What do you mean?" she asked. She began to feel a slight pull behind her stomach.

"One step at a time." Her father said. She couldn't help but notice a hope in his eyes she hadn't seen for years.

Her grandfather leaned forward toward her.

"Wait, what are you doing," she demanded. "I don't want another history lesson right now."

"No, my dear. I will just put the Telum Deos in your hand. There is no chance of harm coming to you. I would never let that happen."

She began to reach out with her right hand and then, changing her mind, putting out her left. Then she took that back and wiped the sweat from her palm on her pants. She tried to make her hands stop shaking. Her grandfather reached into his robe and removed the amulet when her hand was out. It was the same from her vision and what he showed them on the stairs. It looked made of gold or bronze with exquisite markings surrounding it and had a thick chain.

"Wait," Sarah gasped, pulling her hand back as if there was a snake before her. "If that was all true and you are my grandfather, why doesn't anyone else…"

"Sarah, you don't have to call me grandfather; it makes me feel old. What's a couple of two hundred years? My friends called me Renfield or R.M. You will know everything in time. Just relax again. This will not hurt you."

She started to reach out again, relieved to see that her hand was not shaking this time.

"It will be all right, Sarah," her dad added, sitting next to her and resting his hands on her shoulders.

Her grandfather took the amulet and placed it in her hand. It felt cold and heavy. Nothing. Every eye was on it. Sarah felt suddenly silly, wishing that something would happen, or someone would ease the silence with a word.

"Ah!" her grandfather whimpered. A small part of the amulet lit softly, providing no more illumination than a low-energy night light or flashlight.

"It is true!" Renfield cried.

"No," her dad said in disappointment.

"You saw it, didn't you."

"Yes, but it was not enough." Her dad retorted, turning away. Her grandfather rose to face her father. "There is hope! You did see it."

"It was not enough." Her dad snarled.

"What do you mean?" Sarah asked, dropping the amulet.

"The amulet will glow when it is needed. It gives all the gifts needed to fight evil. We placed it in your hand when you were young, and nothing happened. We were unable to have any other children. We shouldn't have believed in this. We should not have gotten our hopes up. We need to prepare for what is coming without fighting it." Her father said as he started to walk toward the stairs, looking moanfully.

"But it lit up before," her grandfather said, following him. "You saw it. It was completely imbued with power again."

"Drop it!" her father called. "It was a mistake to bring Sarah here and show her this."

"What?" Sarah called, getting to her feet.

"You always wanted to give up," her grandfather spat. "Even when you were in the third grade, Wilber boy wanted to fight you. You ran away from him, too."

"Dad, that was years ago and had nothing to do with…"

"Even in potty training, you would rather go in your pants than listen to me."

"He did?" Sarah asked quickly.

"No, I didn't," her father said, looking at Sarah in surprise. Then, looking at his dad, he said, "And I would like you to not speak of this again or to Sarah."

"She is my granddaughter, and she knows now. She is also the last hope we have against…"

"No, she is not!" her dad barked, waving his hands angrily. Sarah took a step back. Seeing her father angry for another day was not something she wanted.

The two bickered on, going nose to nose as she picked up the amulet. It seemed to be calling her. It felt lighter this time in both of her hands. She looked at it closely and turned it over as the other bickered.

"Who could have made this?" she asked herself, looking at the markings upon markings covering it.

"I said put it down!" She heard her dad yell.

She had been so hypnotized by the amulet that she didn't hear the first three times her father told her to put it down. She looked over and saw her father right beside her. He yanked the amulet from her, and she cringed away from him.

"You just want her to be able to when she can't." Her father yelled, shaking the amulet at her grandfather.

"You just won't accept the truth," Renfield yelled back just as loud.

"I won't let her be taken like I lost…" He stopped. Tears now rolling down his cheeks. Unexpectedly, he howled in agony and threw the amulet out the front round window with a crash.

"NO!" her grandfather yelled. In the blink of an eye, he transformed into a bat and flew out of the window. Sarah and her father shared a horrible silence, only distracted by the distant sounds of traffic coming now through the window.

"Sarah, go to your room." Her father ordered, breathing heavily.

"Yes, dad." She said automatically. Her feet felt heavy. The lump in her throat didn't help as she walked to the stairs. She was halfway down when her grandfather flew back into the attic. She saw the long-chain held under his flapping dark wings. Amazed, she saw him transform back into his old self. He was also crying softly now. Her father straightened up and walked toward her to leave. As he passed his father, he hesitated momentarily and reached out a hand toward his shoulder.

"Please go," Renfield said with a sniffle. "You broke. You broke it into four parts. I don't know what we are going to do now. There is nothing like its kind in the world."

"We will do what we were going to do before. We will live our lives as best we can before the end." Her father said, sounding stronger and more resolved.

Not wanting to feel anything else, she descended the stairs, pushed the cabinet, went down the hall, and shut her room door. She couldn't believe that only twenty minutes had gone by. She watched her clock for a moment or two as she curled into a ball on her bed and fell asleep.

"Sarah, we are going to be late," came her father's voice. Her shoulders ached as she stretched the sleep out of them. Why was she so sore? She smacked her lips and made a sour face at the taste of her morning breath. She blew the hair out of her mouth and smiled at the light coming through her window.

"We need to go," her dad said again.

She looked at the clock and saw that she only had five minutes before leaving for school. "Son of a snack bar," she cried, leaping from bed. She whirled through getting ready, and nothing of last night's events returned to her until she emerged into the hallway. She stopped brushing her hair with one hand and buttoning up her shirt with the other. She had her mechanical toothbrush in her mouth as she moved it with her tongue with her hands busy. After a single step in the hallway, she froze, looking down the hall and toward her father's office. A fearful feeling rose from her gut like a deep sour note. The feeling gave her a shiver that caused her toothbrush to fall out of her mouth.

"One minute!"

Her father called again, causing her to roll her eyes. She rushed to get ready as quickly as she could. It wasn't until she went down the stairs that she noticed that she had her skirt on backward, the comb still stuck in her hair, and both shoes on the same foot.

Her father was waiting for her by the door in his worst suit as if this was just another typical morning. When she saw him, she seemed to panic stepping back, and suddenly, she felt hollow and wanted to be anywhere else but with her dad.

He opened his mouth to speak, but before he could say anything, she exclaimed, "Hey, Dad! Look'n Thicc this morn. Breakfast on the go this morning would just be fine, and I don't want to be salty about last night, so let's skurt it for the mo, aight?" Not giving her father a chance to answer, she stumbled out of the house, trying her best to look graceful but failing miserably, walking like she had just had hip surgery.

"Teenagers," her father groaned.

They got in the car and sat for a moment. One buckled and then the other, but still nothing. Every moment was awkward, and every movement was obstructed. It felt like a lifetime of torture just sitting there.

"I have your phone for you." Her dad said, pulling it out of his jacket.

"Ah, yes, good, moral of. You, too, and decent. To give it, it. back, nice, uh, thank you." Sarah said, taking it quickly after saying all that. She buried her head in it, holding it an inch away from her face and still pulling hard to brush her hair. From her father's look, she turned nonplused and acted like she meant to leave the brush in her hair. She felt her father's eyes on her, and he didn't start the car. Minutes passed before he turned it on and slowly drove toward the school. Neither said a word to the other, and the radio was not touched.

Sarah was amazed that none of her friends had posted anything since last night. She knew nothing else was happening until her father asked, "Will that be all right?" She quickly turned around and saw that they were in a drive-through, and he had already ordered something.

"Yeah, yeah, just checking the latest on my squad. So, it's all lit, Dad."

"Uh, all right," he almost sounded like he was whimpering. They moved on, and he handed her a bag of food as they drove away. She didn't know how hungry she was until her food was all gone. Once she finished, she kept her face on her phone. They were almost to their school, and she still didn't know what to do. What was she going to say to her dad or her friends? She didn't want to go to school and didn't want to be home. Thoughts traveled before her mind just as quickly as a breakup post hit the phones.

"Sarah?"

She didn't know what to do. She just sat there as the car rolled to a stop. Her father put the car in park and impatiently grabbed the wheel hard. He started to speak, beating Sarah for a second as she reached for the handle.

"We need to talk," he said quickly.

"Talk," she shouted back, unlocking the doors. "I wanted to talk." She was surprised at how angry she was and how she sounded. "I wanted to talk about this for months, and you didn't want to. So talk to yourself." She opened the door and hurried away.

"SARAH!" her father called, opening the car door. He stood leaning on his open door with one hand and the other on the car's roof. "Sarah, please!"

All the students and parents looked at them both in bewilderment. She walked resolutely toward the school and was swallowed up by the crowd with her head down. She managed to stave off the looks given to her and avoid people through half of her school. Even as she walked out of Miss Amanda's class despite the calls from her teacher to stay, she walked out with a plan. Lunch came, and instead of doing the same thing, she did every day. She went out and sat on the front steps of the school, alone. Kids passed by her, not giving her notice, which is what she wanted.

"If she could only stop thinking," she wished as she counted the cars going by. She barely heard the bell ring, ending lunch. When school ended, she left a note in their car and walked home alone. Her stomach groaned with hunger. She got home, ate, went to her room, and locked the door. She did this for seven days. She did all she could not act, speak, or hear anyone around her for seven days. She would keep her phone turned off for hours, not caring what others posted or said. She deleted the text and didn't answer the door when her father knocked. She didn't attend church or respond to her father's questions. He seemed to ask different things now and then but gave her room.

She sat again for another lunchtime in her spot, watching people go on as if nothing new was happening. She wondered how many of them could have something strange going on that no one knew about when someone suddenly sat beside her.

"So this is where you have been hiding," Shaw said, smiling.

"Go away," Sarah sniffed against the cold, rainy air.

"Go away?" Shaw asked louder than Sarah wanted. Other students took notice. "You are the latest in the homeland security against the paranormal. I don't want to miss anything."

"The paranormal homeland security?"

"Yeah," Shaw said, nodding stupidly. "Jack came up with that one." Then, after the look she gave him, he added, "What we didn't just bump into Martha Stewart in your attic. Although he was just about as pale as she is."

"I don't want to talk about it," Sarah said, lowering her head.

"Talk about it?" Shaw said, straightening his legs. "You don't want to talk about it. You sit out here looking at what the hobos wake up to after the stress test we all went through? Why keep me out of it? What has been going on? Hey, where are you going?" Sarah had started to walk back into the school.

"Sarah," Shaw called following her quickly. "Rach and Jack think I had to use the little boy's room, so I got four point two minutes. We talked and thought it best not to do anything, but I can't let this go by without finding what's fresh. Talk girl."

Sarah hurried to get away, clutching her bookbag against her chest.

"Don't want to talk, huh? I have ways of making you talk." Shaw grabbed her shoulder and stepped in front of her.

"Attention, everyone, please. May I have your attention, please? " Shaw waved his hands in the air. "This will be difficult for you to understand, but I'm saying this out of love."

"Stop it. What are you doing?" Sarah spat uncomfortably, looking around. Everyone was watching them.

"If you will pay attention to our stuartist here, Miss Sarah Fields. She will direct you to the school Twilight Zone because she keeps a living zombie in her attic."

"WHAT?" Sarah cried.

"She will tell you that in case of a monster break out, please take note of your emergency exits, which you will find here and here." He pointed his hands up and down the hallway. "And if there is a sudden drop in air pressure due to the screams of the children that the monsters eat, A club will dispense from the ceiling. Please take it with both hands and defend yourself from the thing with eight eyes.."

"Will you stop it?" Sarah pleaded as the kids around them started to laugh, and some even began applauding.

"Or you can just beat the crap out of the kid who would run faster than you. Leaving him as bait for the monster, allowing you to make off with his girl to safety."

"Stop it," she requested. "I'm begging you."

Shaw acted like he had an invisible baseball bat in his hands. "Once you take your weapon, please defend yourself by aiming for the monster's weak point. We suggest the head, knees, neck, or crotch. And if you are traveling with a minor, please dispatch your monster, then assist the child."

"Stop it, you idiot!" Sarah called one last time, wishing she could melt into the floor.

"If the monster has more than one head, set of knees, necks, or crotch, just pick one that is more convenient for you. The key is not to panic but saver what little life you have left," Shaw said, shrugging.

"All right," Sarah capitulated lowly.

"In case of a tie, two knee, neck, or head hits wins out over one crotch hit," Shaw said, nodding authoritatively with a slight bow.

"All right," Sarah called out louder.

"Just remember, don't stop hitting, and don't exit the jetway until your monster comes to a full and complete stop or no frequent monster miles for you."

"I said all right," Sarah bellowed, pulling on him. "Everyone is watching."

"Everyone is not watching," Shaw said as she pulled him toward the library. "The seventh graders aren't looking. Look at their eyes. They all look stoned. Some of them are backed. He kid with the weave, pay attention to this, it might save your life someday."

"Shut up," Sarah ordered, shoving him into the library.

Shaw stopped laughing as soon as she maneuvered both in the corner of the room and out of earshot. The kids in the hallway started applauding and returned to what they were doing.

"Ok, tell me what is going on," Shaw said, leaning forward excitedly, looking Sarah in the eye. "I mean, my life before this happened was Droopy Dog, and now it's like a cross of Sylvester Stallone and Van Helsing."

"Nothing is happening," Sarah said, angrily pushing Shaw hard in the chest. Shaw didn't say anything surprising for a moment. Sarah seemed to pace in a circle for a moment.

"Nothing is happening," Sarah repeated, sounding almost like she was going to cry. Shaw watched her leaning on a book shelve. Neither said anything for a moment until it all came out of Sarah.

"I haven't talked to my dad, you, or anyone," she said, whimpering. She started to cry and lowered her head. She couldn't see through the tears but knew it was Shaw's shoulder that she felt support her and his hands patting her back.

For the first time, Shaw looked uncomfortable. Looking around, he saw a kid sitting down at the end of the bookshelf with large glasses, staring at them.

"Uh, hey," Shaw said, waving at the kid. He pulled his arms away from Sarah as if she were on fire. Sarah suddenly pulled away.

"That's just Stanly," she wiped her nose and tears. "It's all right, he's deaf."

"Yes, because if this were happening in any other situation, it would be weird," Shaw said dully.

"Can I go now?" Sarah said, sniffing.

"Come on, you have to give me something after all," Shaw said excitedly. "I need something new to tell my therapist. Come out of that birdcage. Please send me your fan mail. I can't go back and unsee that window into coolness from my dull life. I tried some stuff, and it didn't work. Don't eat six bowls of candy, by the way with three DynaPep boasts, whooow."

"Shaw, please stop."

"**Are you** telling me you haven't done anything since then? You're in the weird, I'm out. Come on, clock me in." Shaw said in disgust.

"SSsshhhhh!" The librarian sounded behind the counter, making her glasses droop lower on her slender nose. Shaw pulled Sarah away from the librarian, giving her a dirty look.

"Sarah, you can't…" Shaw stopped talking, seeing that he had stopped right in front of Stanly. "Go take care of your glands and overactive sphincter somewhere else." Stanly shook his head, not understanding. "Get lost! Go hit yourself with a hammer. Nerd Nerd man go away come back some other never." Shaw finished the last part, mouthing each word slowly, exaggerating each syllable, moving closer to Stanly until their noses touched. Stanly quickly gathered his books and tried to walk away but slammed into another book shelve. Books clamored to the ground loudly. Stanly didn't bother to pick them up but tried to walk away as if nothing happened.

"I'm dying here! I need new abnormal input." Shaw said seriously. He was holding Sarah by her shoulders, looking her in the eye. "It's been like a mental prison here, not knowing anything except what I saw that night. That wasn't some strange prank, was it?"

… "Yeah," Sarah looked up at the ceiling. "Jack got it all, and we were going to post it, but it was too dark."

"That's not true!" Jack shouted from behind the book shelve. It seemed Rachael and he were hiding just out of view, listening in.

"Sssshh!" The Librarian ordered again angrily. All four of them looked from the angry librarian and moved further away into another corner of the library.

"Don't try and pass this on me," Jack retorted.

"Not so loud," Rachael whispered urgently. "She can get so mad that her hair uncurls. I remember the time someone returned a book torn in half. You would think it was a baby, and she picked the wrong answer from Judge Solomon."

The other three paused their argument, looking at Rachael, clearly not understanding what she had just said.

"WHAT?" Rachael spat in protest.

"SSHHH," Shaw, Sarah, and Jack said together, checking to see if she was heard. Jack had even gone so far as to cover her mouth.

Seeing they were overlooked, Jack whispered, "What is happening? I thought we agreed to give her time. And what was that thing we all saw?"

Not caring if they were noticed, Shaw said at average volume. "I couldn't wait any more. And what was that thing you trapped me with."

"I deserve to know as well. Thank you very much." Rachael said vigorously, folding her arms.

Sarah wished she could escape, but there was nowhere to go. They had her in a corner, and her chest hurt with each breath. The three of them watched her. She opened her mouth and then closed it. Then she thought about where she would go. These were her only close friends. The school didn't feel the same, and her home didn't feel the same either. Where could she go to get away from all of this?

"Sarah," Jack said, placing a hand on her shoulder. "We are here for you. You know that, right? Since we all first met and learned, we were facing the same hard time. We promised to be there for each other." Jack stepped in front of her, but Sarah kept her heavy head down. She didn't want to look at them.

"We are here for you," all three said together, just as they had before. Someone else put their arms around her. Their arms were gentle and kind. Sarah knew that it was Rachael. Suddenly, someone else hugged them all, almost knocking them over. That was Shaw not caring or seeming out of place.

"Just give me one more day," Sarah said, sounding stronger. This was not an act. She felt stronger as a tiny warmth was growing in her stomach.

"Ok," Rachael said, sounding like she was addressing a group of teachers. "We will be here if you need us, but we will give you twenty-four hours, and then we will intervene, all right?" She padded Sarah on the back.

"And you," She thundered. "We want to talk to you." She had grabbed Shaw by the ear and pulled him off them.

"Ouch!" He cried like a small, wounded pig in complaint.

"I know we talked about waiting till she was ready. Why did you bother her without telling us? You were supposed to give her time. You little abnormal social parasite."

"Let him go, or she will get us," Jack cried, but it was too late. From behind a bookshelf aisle came the librarian. Her face was as red as her hair and dangerously uncurled appearing like flames of anger from her scalp.

"I told you to be quiet!" She bellowed.

"Scatter!" Shaw cried. He made a break for it back down their aisle with Rachael still hanging on to his ear, trying to explain that they were looking for a book. She was still holding on to Shaw as tight as a sea crab's claw. Jack grabbed Sarah and bolted to the left of the aisle as Shaw and Rachael went right. Shaw's scream of pain grew louder like a wounded parrot as he tried to get away, pulling Rachael like a fisherman on a line hooked to his ear all the way out of the library. Jack led Sarah out of the other exit of the library and safely into the sea of students in the hallway.

Chapter Seven

The Blood Sucking Care Bear

Jack and Sarah didn't say anything as they parted ways in the hall. She didn't know what to say either. Their eyes said everything they both needed to know. Jack's eyes told of his concern while Sarah's showed the anxiety-like waves from the sea of emotion that kept pounding her continually. Sarah barely made it to her classes and only thought of what the teachers were saying vaguely. Every time she looked at the clock, the only thought in her mind was what she would do. What if she did nothing and lied to her friends? That was what she decided to do during English class. She would sit down and force her dad to tell her everything, had dawned on her halfway through Science. She was almost done with her last period when she changed her mind again and was going to walk home to give her more time to think.

There were five minutes to go when her teacher's phone rang. "Sarah Fields, you must take your things to the office," her teacher said. There was a general moaning of jealousy among all the other students. Sarah walked with her head down to her locker and then to the office.

The office secretary was busy talking to another parent on the other side of her desk. They seemed to be talking for a long time, so she sat down. There was only one other student in the waiting room. She had seen him before but didn't know his name. He was somewhat overweight; his clothes bulged under his girth from sitting down.

Feeling out of place more by the minute, she wished again to go away. She hadn't noticed that she closed her eyes until her chair moved unexpectedly.

"I'm Eric, hi."

She let out a small squawk of fright. The large boy had plopped down right next to her. She could hear her skin crawl as she took in all the features of his round face. His hair was cut very short, showing dips and bumps in his scalp.

"What?" she asked. She coughed to try and cover up the fact that her voice was shaky.

'I'm Eric,' he said again in the same gray tone as before, as if he were an annoying recording. ' You are just like me.'

"What?" She said louder this time. What in the world would she have in common with this guy?

"You are in trouble?" His smile widened, making his eyes almost disappear. "Are you in trouble?"

"No, I was called down. Don't know why."

"Uh, my dad is talking to the counselor again. It seems I caused another problem. Thought you may have heard."

It took all the strength that she had to try and ignore him.

"Did you hear?"

"Hear what?" she asked, sliding to the other side of her chair to avoid him rubbing against her.

"What I did?"

"No."

"Ah, give it time." He sniffed, raising his arms behind his head. It was difficult work. "Everyone will hear soon enough."

The large clock above them ticked away each second louder and louder as Sarah started to grind her teeth.

"Do you want to know what I did?"

"No, no, thank you."

"Ok, I won't tell you…Well, perhaps just a little. Oh, maybe half Fine, I'll tell you." He leaned forward, causing the bench to shift again. "I am not going to sugarcoat it, but I am a little large for my age."

"Right." She sniveled, sliding dangerously on the edge of her chair to get further away from him.

"Gym shorts, and I have grievances. We were playing ball and Greg, you know Greg? The tall kid thinks he's better than me just because he can afford those potions of beauty products that won't work on me because of my overactive facial sweat glands. Anyway, He ain't all that. I would have won that kissing contest if they counted all the ladies on the other side of my computer screen. He's so jealous that he tried to swipe the ball away from me and hit my shorts. Well, they fell."

"So?"

"I was in such a hurry changing in the locker room that I forgot to put on my…"

"Eric." A school counselor called from around the corner.

"Expect you will hear about it soon enough. A lot of ladies won't be able to sleep tonight in lust with that image in their head." He got up to alleviate the pressure on the bench seat he was in. "Good luck with your problem, which you were too shy to share." He said, walking away. "If you tell them you'll run away from home, the school counselors always sympathize with you. Gets you out of any jam." Those were the last words he said before all of him went around the corner.

…. "Wow." She said to herself.

"Sarah dear?" the secretary said as the man she was talking with left the office.

"Your father left this note for you," she said, searching for it underneath her piles. Her desk was untidy, and she had to answer the phone asking people to hold it three times before finding it. She handed it to her and waved her off.

"Sarah," she read. "I have been called away urgently. Miss Amanda will give you a ride home. I should be back by 9. We will talk then. Love you, Dad." She read it three times before it sunk in. Her father had never done this before.

The bell rang, and she followed the crowds of kids leaving the school. She was dizzyingly walking toward the parking lot. She saw Jack coming out of the west exit. He was hurrying toward his mother, waiting in their car. Sarah started to jog toward him but slowed, seeing she wouldn't catch him before he got in the car. Just as he was getting in, he saw her. He raised a hand, telling her to wait, and gave her a thumbs up and an ok sign before they drove off.

"What does that mean?" she said, feeling alone, resting her hands on her hips.

"Sarah?" Miss Amanda called. She was leaving the school, holding a large bag under her shoulder. She already drew the looks of most of the guys who were of the age to be more stupid than usual. But if she were to get in the car with her? That would be enough to make the rest of her days in Lon Chaney Jr. High worse than daily dental visits.

"Over here, Sarah." She called again.

"I can't hear you. Kids are messing with my head too loud."

"Don't be silly." Miss Amanda called, hurrying over to her.

"OOoooowwww," all the kids sounded around her.

"Hey," came that annoying voice again. It was Eric hurrying over to her. Well, as fast as his hurrying could be.

Sarah actually let out a small cry when she saw him.

"Come on, hurry." Miss Amanda said, grabbing her arm. "Run, don't walk away from him."

Sarah felt an overwhelming feeling of relief. Miss Amanda didn't seem to be a teacher anymore as she opened the door to her car for her.

"Nice car," Sarah said without thinking. "What is it?"

Miss Amanda was putting her bag in the back. It's a 1969 Mustang; hurry, get in. He's still coming."

"You dare bring *this* to a school?" Sarah mumbled as she opened the door and climbed in.

Once in, they began to drive away. They went a few blocks when Sarah felt that she should say something.

"Thank you for the ride, Miss Amanda."

"You can forget the Miss for now. If you can keep a secret."

"What?"

"Just call me Amanda and leave the Miss at school. Amanda is my first name. My last name is Johansson, but Johansson almost sounds like a Y chromosome name."

"What about the miss at the front of that?"

"Hey, it's a new time, which could mean many different things. Do you know why your dad called in this favor?" Amanda asked.

"No, I thought you knew."

"Hmm, No. I assumed he would have told you something."

They drove quickly to her house. It was different to be driven by someone other than her father. Dozens of questions filled her head as they went on. What was her father doing? Why couldn't she walk home like she did most of the time her father was busy? What did Jack mean? The last question she thought of didn't stay in her head as a new one popped in and out of her mouth.

"How do you know where I live?" She asked.

"You don't know?" Amanda asked, swerving a little suddenly. "Your dad hasn't told you?"

"No, told me what?"

"It's best if it comes from your dad."

Sarah was thinking fast. There was so much going on. What could she mean? Did Amanda have something to do with the Telum Deos, her grandfather, or was this about her project?

"Oh, that," Sarah said, sounding more confident than she really was. "Yeah, my dad and I talked about that."

"Really, I thought he would want me there when he did. I hope you are all right with it so far?"

"All right? With what?" she thought. If she was talking about learning that her family had been fighting the armies of darkness, and she was supposed to be the next recruit but was somehow failing? Then how could anyone be all right with that?

"It takes some getting used to..." She said, hoping that playing it in the middle would work. "I mean, it's not a Trump kind of problematic thing. You know?"

"What?" Amanda asked, not understanding, turning down their street.

"Uhh," Sarah gasped. "Uhh, I'm going to run away from home."

"What, really?" Amanda cried, slamming on the breaks.

"No, no, no," Sarah cried, wishing she had not blurted out the first thing that came to her mind. "I am just not going to be able to unsee that tonight. Amanda, I'm sorry. I'll just get out here. It's all right. I was told there would be days like this, but that was a little much. Do you feel me? You had a mother." Sarah said all this very quickly.

"Yeahhh," Amanda said weakly.

Sarah got out quickly but started to shut the door, opened it, almost shut it, and repeated this four times before finishing with, "It's complicated." She closed the door a little too hard and hurried home.

Shutting her house door behind her, she stood still momentarily with her back to the door. She didn't realize it, but she was there for almost twenty minutes, holding her face in her hands. She slid to the floor, lowering her head between her knees, not thinking, wishing she couldn't feel anything. She stayed there, not caring for anything, until her stomach reminded her she was hungry. When she got up, she was surprised to feel her cheeks were wet. She opened the fridge and instinctively took some food and some out of cabinets. She was halfway up the stairs when she saw down the hall. A cold chill ran down her back. She slowed until she opened her door and rushed in, shutting it quickly and locking it behind her.

She was thankful that all she felt was hunger. Setting her things down, she flopped on her bed and turned on her television. She didn't even look what was on as Star Trek started playing. She was making a mess when she unexpectedly heard a thumping sound. Searching for the remote under the plastic wrappers and fumbling to hit mute. Straining her ears, she heard it again. The only thing that moved was her eyes. She wanted to know what that was but didn't want to know. It would stop and then come again and again. Then it was gone. She put her half-eaten Twinkie down and leaned to the edge of her bed.

Nothing

Wham! Something hit her window behind her, causing her to scream. She saw in her mind the image of a vampire bat must have slammed into the glass. She grabbed the lamp beside her bed and held it over her head as a weapon. She slowly inched closer and closer toward her window until she was an inch away when, Wham!

She screamed again louder and jumped. Someone was throwing something at her window. Opening her window quickly, she saw, "Jack? What are you doing?"

"You haven't been answering your phone! You, ok?" he called up.

"My phone!?!" she felt in her pocket and, with horror, discovered it was gone.

"Are you all right?" Jack called again. "Yeah, sorry, I don't know where my phone is. Hey, what are you throwing?"

"I was worried if I threw rocks, I would break your window, so I grabbed some diapers from your neighbor's trash cans. Let us in."

Sarah was halfway across her room before she slowed, understanding what Jack had just told her. Shaking her head, she hurried down to open the door to Jack, Rachael, and Shaw. They didn't come in but stood outside.

"What?" Sarah asked, peeking her head around the door.

"Is your dad here?" Jack asked feebly.

"No, he won't be back till tonight."

"Good!" Shaw called. He pushed past the other two strongly.

"Good?" Rachael puffed. "You hid behind me ever since we turned down the street. When did you take bravery pills?"

"Who needs pills?" Shaw said, looking around the house, trying to appear that he was not looking for Sarah's dad. "I'm imbued with bravery."

"You sure were when you were stuck upstairs," Jack said with a smile. Shaw only rolled his eyes.

"We were so worried when you didn't answer our calls, texts, posts, tweets, emails, and pages," Rachael said, breathing more manageable now.

"What?"

"We were worried," Shaw called defensively.

"Yeah, and we wanted to make sure your dad wouldn't be here if we came over," Jack said again, almost laughing at Shaw's face.

Sarah shut the door, and Jack and Rachael looked at each other as if neither knew what to say or how to say what was on their minds.

"So, how is the man upstairs?" Shaw said humorously.

"Ahhh, Shaw," Rachael and Jack both said in disgust. "Tactfully, tactfully, man. We talked about that, come on." Jack finished.

"Why are you picking on me? You two weren't doing anything."

"There is so much wrong with you and your mind," Rachael said, shaking her head and closing her eyes in abhorrence.

"I've learned to live with it," Shaw smirked. "What is going on? You have to tell me something. You are living a nerd's dream! Give me something, feed me."

"Shaw, nothing is going on, and nothing will be going on," Sarah said, feeling very tired.

There was a soft banging sound again that Sarah heard before.

"What was that?" They all asked together.

Then, they all spoke at the same time. "Who did that?" Jack asked, looking around. "Sounds like someone is knocking?" came from Rachael. "I thought that was you before," Sarah said, turning white. "Finally," Shaw exclaimed excitedly.

"Sarah, you are coming with us," Jack ordered as the bumping and thumping resumed. He pushed past the girls and grabbed the door. It wouldn't open. He pulled and jerked, but nothing happened.

"Your, door, is stuck." He said between tugs.

"It's probably just because of the rain we had," Rachael said smartly.

"It's never done that before." Sarah sounded afraid.

"It's because of the thumper," Shaw said breathlessly. He looked as if it were Christmas.

"Thumper?" Rachael asked, shutting her eyes again as if Shaw's words had hurt her. As they pulled on the door, Sarah and Jack didn't notice.

"Haven't any of you seen a scary movie before?" Shaw said, pulling the three others to look at him. "The good-looking girl is always taken, and then the hero's sidekick before they discover what is killing them. So you girls are safe, but Jack, I'm afraid you're done for."

Rachael and Sarah rolled their eyes at the insult, but Jack clearly didn't get it.

"Go for the back door." Rachael sang out, pushing Shaw hard out of the way.

The thumping grew louder, causing all four to stop searching for where it was coming from. It appeared to be reverberating from all around them. It was growing louder and stronger. Sarah let out a squill and started to jog to her back door. Jack and Rachael followed, but the door wouldn't budge. She slammed her shoulder on the door when the beating stopped.

"Now what?" Rachael asked.

"The window!" Jack pointed.

"Wait," Sarah roared. "Where is Shaw?"

They all turned from the window to look around. Shaw was nowhere to be found. They all called for him, and each started to go their way. Jack grabbed both girls' shoulders.

"We should stay together," he exclaimed, breathing heavily from worry. They all called for him to retrace their steps.

"Shaw! Shaw?" Rachael screamed. She was the first to see him by the bookshelves; they all passed by the stairs. Shaw stood upright and moved like a marionette as they had just seen him move the book that released the door upstairs.

"Shaw, NO!" Jack shrieked, pushing forward down the hall toward him. Shaw turned toward them but took no notice and began to go up the stairs, grabbing the handrail. Before he took his first step, Jack lowered his shoulder into him to tackle him, but it was as if Jack had hit a brick wall. He fell to the floor, and it did absolutely nothing to Shaw.

The girls hurried to Jack's aid. "I'm all right," Jack whimpered as they helped him to his feet. He rubbed his shoulder as they looked up, watching Shaw move robot-like off the stairs up the hall.

"Stop him!" Sarah called. They all sprinted after him up the stairs, but once they got to the top, they hit an invisible wall. Rachael was the first and toppled back on the other two. Sarah fell under the weight of the other two as she slowed their fall down the stairs, stopping them halfway down.

"What was that?" Rachael whimpered, rubbing her head and hip where she had hit.

"We have to stop him!" Sarah said, pulling her apart from the other two and ascending the stairs again. This time, she slowed before hitting the invisible barrier and felt for it. Nothing was there.

"Shaw, stop!" She saw him turn into her father's office.

She moved down the hallway as quickly as she could with her hand held out, readying herself to be hit with whatever invisible force obstructed them. Jack and Rachael followed closely behind them. Sarah would have felt stupid on any other day the way she was walking past her room. Her arms outstretched, knees bent, as if she were playing blind man's bluff without a blindfold. It would have been even better if she could see her friends behind her, who looked even stupider. She hit the invisible barrier at the door to the office.

"Shaw, stop, don't go up there." Shaw's foot just disappeared up the stairs to the secret room.

"I'll stop him," Jack said as all three pushed against the invisible wall. "You two go for help."

"I'm not leaving him or you." Sarah gasped, pushing as hard as she could.

"All right," Rachael said as she turned back the way they came. She went two feet before she hit another unseen obstruction.

"Were trapped!" She cried, grabbing the knee that hit it first. All three hit, pushed, and shoved, but nothing happened.

"AAAAHHHHHhhhh! Someone cried, causing all three to freeze. Their blood ran cold as they looked at each other.

"Was that Shaw?" Jack asked lowly.

"SHAW?" Sarah yelled. She went to push against her barrier but fell again to the floor. It was gone. Jack jumped over her while Rachael helped Sarah and followed. They were all calling Shaw's name. They ran up the stairs and saw Shaw on the floor next to the table, rolling on the floor in a fetal position.

"Shaw?" Shaw, are you all right? Don't be dead," they all said.

Jack was the first to reach him and pulled him on his back. Nothing they had seen would prepare them for what they witnessed.

"You idiot!" Jack yelled, striking Shaw in the stomach.

Shaw was laughing so hard he was double up rolling on the floor.

"He's all right?" Sarah and Rachael said together.

"You should have seen yourselves charge up those stairs." Shaw gasped hysterically.

"He's ok!" Rachael breathed in relief.

"I came out of that trance as soon as I got up here. Ha ha, ha, heeeeeeeeeeeeeeeeeee, and then I, I, haaaaaaaahe. I told him what if I screamed," Shaw said, wiping tears of laughter out of his eyes as he snorted. "He told me it was stupid, but I did it anyway, and you three ran up here like you caught your parents kissing downstairs."

"I'll kill him!" Rachael yelled, charging forward and kicking at him with Jack and Sarah holding her back. Shaw only laughed more before Jack pushed both girls back and cried, "Wait, wait, who did you tell you were going to scream."

Sarah, Shaw, and Rachael slowed and became paralyzed as fear swept over them. Shaw was still laughing as the other three looked up from him. The room was just as it was when Sarah was last in it, except for the lone figure standing in the far corner.

Jack stepped forward in front of Sarah, shielding her as Rachael slowly retreated. Shaw let out a small gasp of what Sarah thought was fear. It turns out they each looked at the dark figure. Shaw stopped laughing and was in pain because Jack had stepped on his hand.

"We can't get out!" Rachael sniveled. She was pushing against another invisible wall, keeping them from escaping.

"No, no, no, please," Shaw moaned.

"Yeah, don't hurt us," Jack spat, pushing Sarah back. She twisted to see if it was her grandfather, but Jack kept trying to protect her.

"Ouch, Ahh!" Jack yelled. Sarah and Rachael jumped and screamed. Shaw had taken a mouse trap with his free hand and snapped it to Jack's leg, which was standing on his hand.

"He's not going to hurt us!" Shaw roared, getting to his feet. He held his hands to calm them down. "I'm sorry, sorry! Ok?" If I knew you were going to freak out. I wouldn't have done it." Shaw started rubbing his hurt hand. Then, shrugging, he added, "Ok, I probably would still have done it, but he will not hurt us. Just calm down."

"How do you know?" Jack asked as he jumped on one leg, pulling off the trap on his other.

"I won't hurt any of you," the voice said in the corner. He said it so softly that he had to repeat it three times before they noticed and stopped arguing. It also didn't help that Rachael was still slapping Shaw.

"What do you want?" Sarah gasped.

"And if you don't hurt us, let us out of here!" Rachael called finishing one last hard slap at Shaw.

"Done," Renfield said, waving a hand before him.

"Is that how you do it?" Jack inquired.

"No, I just thought it was a cool Skywalker thing," Renfield added. "Can you believe the end of episode nine?" He sounded so excited suddenly.

"What?" all four asked at the same time in confusion.

"I'm sorry to break the mood here. Uh, I needed to talk to you."

Sarah pushed Jack out of the way. Unfortunately, he was still on one foot. He fell to the ground, triggering two more mouse traps on his hand and elbow.

Ignoring his screams, Sarah growled, "Then let my friends go and ask me what you want."

"No," Renfield said, taking a small step forward. His voice was not angry or ordering but pleading. They could see him a little better, showing that he wore scrubs with Mickey ears and fluffy slippers. "I wish to address you and your companions. It is of the utmost importance that we converse as a group. In your language, it's a Thanos Endgame thing."

"What?" They all looked dumb-struck and bewildered.

After calming them down, he moved things off the coffee table with a wave of his hand again. He sat down on the place he made and asked them to sit down. Sarah urged them to do so and ensured they would be all right. Rachael was the last to do so, but he began once they were all placed. He told them everything that they informed Sarah the other night. He didn't hypnotize them but explained it clearly.

"Why are you telling us?" Rachael asked when he was done.

"Don't have him start," Shaw spat quickly. "You'll mess with his head, and I want him to keep going. I mean, wow, man."

"I wish I could impress upon your consciousness of the importance of the message I wish to deliver. The reflections are coming, and new blood is required."

"If you are going to suck my blood, use a straw!" Shaw spat, sitting back suddenly in fear.

"No, no," Renfield cried. "I don't do that. Just small vermin is what I require, and I keep the house free of pests." His words calmed them down, as well as his warm face. "I speak of free blood."

Rachael raised her hand as if she was in class, "We do not understand."

"The reflections are coming, and you four, somehow, have the new blood for the Telum Deos. Darkness is growing. He is here somewhere." Renfield waved his hands at the constellations drawn on the ceiling and newspaper clippings on the walls.

"I get that you have had something strange happen to you and a soap opera series past with a little Game of Thrones thrown in there, but I still don't get what that means to us," Jack said.

"You three are very quick to believe all this," Rachael stated oddly.

Renfield rubbed his head as Rachael explained that something else may have happened to explain everything downstairs, with Renfield holding up a hand.

"Perhaps?" he said. He wanted them to take it. Shaw reached quickly, taking it.

"What?" he asked at the strange looks the other three were giving him. "Calm up, John Wayne up."

Sarah was next, followed quickly by Jack. Rachael did but then took it back quickly.

"What are you going to do?"

"I shall not bring harm to you," Renfield said, smiling with a nod.

Her hand was shaking as she reached it out. She was an inch away when it slowed. Shaw leaned over, grabbed it, and placed it with theirs.

Boom! It was as if they were all being sucked down a tube. It was the same experience as Sarah had before being hypnotized, but she knew that Jack, Rachael, and Shaw were with her. The darkness turned and swirled about them until they stopped on some dark stage. They were there but without form, as

Renfield's voice sounded over a loudspeaker. "About every seventy-five years, the comet comes close to our world." Out of the darkness, a comet appeared and flew inches over them. Stars followed as they followed the comet through space.

"As it comes, the forces of darkness grow in strength," Renfield said over the wisps and zings of things they passed: planets, moons, stars. In the distance, they could see Earth.

"As it grows closer, light from our sun hits it in such a way that it reflects on the crystal they launched so many years ago, which we have been unable to find. When it aligns, a light brings the evil around Dracula's location, giving him strength and a sample of his power. We don't know the intricacies between the crystal and the comet. All we know is the results that we fight."

They watched as their perception changed from being on the comet to a beam of light from their sun. They traveled instantly from the sun back to the comet, to the large crystal orbiting the earth back down to where they sat.

They sat gasping wildly, holding onto their seats, except for Shaw.

"Again!" He exclaimed, waving his hand out in front of him. "Again, do me, do me, just me."

"This is real," Rachael whispered in shock, rubbing her temples. She said it over and over again.

"If this crystal is causing a problem, why doesn't the military just blow it away," Jack asked, shaking his head.

"You have no idea what he is capable of," Renfield said. He seemed to be more relaxed as all of them seemed more comfortable. "He can be anyone and control countless people. For all we know, entire nations are serving him. Trust me, I know."

"All right," Jack went on. "Then why haven't you just gotten some A-Team together and taken care of it yourselves?"

"The crystal is lost somewhere, and we have done all we could to find it. I have tried for centuries to locate it, but not knowing its weight or rate of thrust, we have been unable to determine its trajectory or location. We have to discover it by following the results it brings. We are just controlling the damage it brings. That's all we have been able to do." Renfield lowered his head and reached into his scrub pocket. "Until now."

"Wait," Rachael said quickly. "If the danger is here now? Why haven't we seen any of it?"

"You have!" Renfield kept his hand in his pocket. He seemed to treat Rachael a little gentler than Jack and Shaw. "You just haven't known the reason."

"The blackout," Sarah said in surprise. Renfield smiled as she went on. "The furless animals, toys coming to life."

"That is just a glimpse of what we have been struggling to deal with our own meager forces."

"Us?" Rachael asked when she stopped rubbing her head. "Why tell us?"

Renfield took something out of his robe. Light shined between his fingers. All their eyes watched as he held it out before him and opened his hand. All four parts of the Telum Deos were there, glowing green. The pieces were situated as if they had just broken and easily could have been glued together.

"That's the amulet you told us about?" Jack asked with the green reflecting in his eyes.

"Yes," Renfield said. "Our weapon to wield for peace. It will grant its wearers with strength, speed, and the means for defense and attack. "The Telum Deos is calling for its new champion."

"But that's, Sarah," Rachael exclaimed. She didn't sound afraid anymore.

"No," Renfield said, raising his hand higher so the light showed across the room. "Only one part was shown when Sarah was near it last. When all four of you enter the house, it reflects the purity of intent the four of you can possess. It is calling not to one of you but all. It has chosen you."

All four gave a very different response. "Sweet," Shaw said. "How would that work," Rachael asked. "You mean this intense mood ring thing knew we were in the house?" came from Jack. Sarah sat up, "What do you mean the four of us? You do not mean what I think you mean?"

"Yes," Renfield "Never have four been chosen. You might be the means to bring about the end of Dracula and his power. You are our only hope, champions, and the new blood."

They all stayed still for a moment, taking in what this meant in their own ways.

"Dude, sweet," Shaw said, nodding his head. "This is going to be the coolest thing on a resume. And I would just like to say I am happy to be a part of this Whatever it is. You're like a scary care bear that comes with a prize."

Jack, Sarah, and Rachael stared at him again, not believing what they just heard.

"What?" is all Shaw said.

Chapter Eight

I Motion We Close the Meeting and Call It a Night

"Might we take a moment for clarification purposes?" Rachael asked with unease and hesitation in her voice.

"Clarification purposes?" Sarah panted. "Clarification? Rachael, really?" Then she turned on Renfield. "All you told me was that I was in a line of vampire fighters, and for some reason, I am not good enough. But now you want my friends to fight. You want all four of us to fight?"

"Yes, you must." Renfield nodded with resolve.

"No," Sarah groaned. "I don't want this. I don't want this for them. I don't even know if I believe any of this."

"Sarah," Jack moved forward in his seat. "I don't understand, but I don't think I have to believe. It seems like it's just a point of responsibility."

Sarah sat up quickly. "Responsibility? What if one of us gets hurt? What if someone we know gets hurt or killed? I can't live with that. I can't even live with my grades."

"Oh, come on," Shaw fell back, slouching in his chair. "It's easy not to care about grades. I don't know the last grade I cared about. Come to think about it, I don't know what grade I even looked at."

"They are most likely further down the alphabet than you can say…" Jenifer said sharply.

"Despite what you want, reality is pressing upon you, and your lives will be forever changed before this day. You do not have a choice about whether you are involved. All you can do is respond to the threat which has presented itself. All you can choose is how you will respond. Evil is out there, and it is coming." Renfield stated, lowering his head.

"What do you mean it is coming?" Rachael asked. She sounded like she was a little more straightforward.

"When the light of darkness shines," Renfield did not lift his head when he spoke. "The evil that was infused in it before breaks out, partly, to whatever it shines on." "Oh yeah, that makes sense," Shaw said, taking out his phone and starting to play on it.

"Not now," Rachael yelled, slapping it out of his hands. "And sit up!"

"The power of the crystal can bring evil life to whatever it shines on." Renfield rose spookily as if he were floating. He started to pace to a side of the room with newspaper clippings of oddities.

"Here are some of the things we have dealt with in the past," he said, pointing at different clippings. "February 2, 1953. In Russia, there was this evil attack on a group of skiers. All the people found of them was a torn apart tent, traces of radioactivity, and there was no sign of what caused their deaths."

Renfield moved on to the next, "Earlier still the Mary Celeste ship was off the coast of Azores in 1872. The ship was completely intact, but all 400 souls on board were gone without a trace."

He moved eagerly to other random sections of information on the walls. "The Voynich manuscript, in 2010 Beebe Arkansas

5,000 blackbirds suddenly died, In Taos New Mexico there is a Hum that is heard that no one can explain that drives the hearers mad. In Flannan Isles of Scotland, in December 1900, everyone had disappeared, and all the clocks had stopped at the same time, the disappearance of Malaysia Airlines flight 370, 239 people gone, Loch Ness, Sasquatch, The Bermuda Triangle…"

He was now flying across the room, pointing to different sections of papers, "the Tunguska Siberia loss of 820 miles of trees 110 years ago. The Nazca Lines…."

"Grandfather!" Sarah yelled.

Renfield froze. He was zipping across the room in a blur so quickly that papers started to be pulled off the walls. He looked at all four of them, seeing that they were afraid. Not from what he was saying but fearful of him.

"I apologize," he said, falling to the floor and stepping back. "My solitarily brings side effects I do not realize. I ask you for your forgiveness."

Sarah sat back down, not taking her eyes off him. Jack broke the tense silence. "How do we stop it?" His voice sounded heavy, as if something was stuck in his throat.

Sarah and Rachael looked at Jack angrily. Shaw smirked and nodded his head slowly. Renfield raised his sheepish head slightly but did not advance toward them.

"Once the crystal shines and a connection is made. You must find the original evil and break the connection made before it spreads out of control."

"Spreads? Rachael asked inquisitively.

"Just like all evil, it grows. It begins with one and then spreads from there. You must find the first change from the darkness and stop it. That will destroy all the ones it has infected."

"What you are saying is," Renfield cut Rachael off, moving quickly deeper into the corner.

"Oh, good!" He cried, falling to his knees.

"Uhhh," Rachael said, craning her neck and raising her eyebrows to see what he was doing.

There was a sickening, crunching noise as Renfield got to his feet and slowly walked toward them. As he crossed the light from the window, they saw that he was chowing on something, and three spider legs were out of the side of his mouth.

"I hear your father's car coming," Renfield said, smacking his lips. "He should arrive in about twenty minutes, depending on the lights. You must go but ponder the urgency that has come to you with haste."

"Right," Shaw said, getting up quickly and looking for his phone. "Next time, my place. Good to meet you, Reiny, don't eat any Italian food without me?' He picked up his phone and started to walk out. Jack helped Sarah to her feet and walked beside her, with Rachael following, keeping them between her and Renfield.

"Sarah, a word for a moment," Renfield asked.

Shaw hopped down the stairs, and Rachael hurried past Renfield as Jack held his hand to her for assistance. Jack didn't leave Sarah until she nodded toward him, letting him know to go. "Wait for me downstairs," she said.

Once they went down the stairs, Renfield moved closer to her. She took a step back instinctively. He stopped and instantly looked awkward. He looked like he was six years old suddenly and scared to tell a grown-up that he had made a mess.

"Sarah, take these and give them to your friends. They may need them." Renfield handed her the broken pieces of the Telum Deos Amulet. Three parts were dimmer than when she first saw them, and one part was still bright.

When she took them, Renfield smiled, "Sarah, I didn't want this for you, but you and your friends are the world's only hope. You will never know what you have till it is taken away. The way of life in this world is at stake. I have lived over a hundred years and seen much, but nothing is more beautiful than you are. Witnessing the wars between your countries has brought horrible events to end life, but what we are fighting is a war on a global scale. Don't doubt yourself or the enemy. They wish to extinguish all life or bring it under their control. Your father must never know we spoke." His smile faltered as a tear started to fall down his face. He looked away and waved for her to go.

She felt something now. It was as if she hadn't felt anything for the past hour. Inside her came a new tiny seed of pity. She found her hand coming up and wiping away his tears. His face was cold to the touch and didn't feel like skin. The shock brought her to her senses as she turned to go. She hesitated after her first step. She opened her mouth to say something, but nothing came out. Her grandfather was still turned away. Taking a deep breath, she went down.

As she reached the last step, Renfield said, "Don't tell your father you were up here. He doesn't understand and always remember, I love you."

Her last step faltered. She didn't know how to take that. She turned back to look up the stairs. They were empty as she heard him walking to the couch on the other side of the room.

"I won't tell him." She called up as she moved the bookcase back.

The walk down the hall and to the front room seemed to take longer than before. Everyone else was sitting in her front room. Their whispering stopped, and they jumped to their feet as soon as they saw Sarah.

"You ok?" Jack asked quickly.

"Sure, she is fine," Shaw stated excitedly. "I don't see no hickey with two holes on her, and besides, it's not every day you learn your grandpa is a member of the undead. Mine has looked dead for the last two years, but they're still walking. And you get to kick some serious monster back two cheeks with the same promise of those PF flyers."

"There is a great deal to process here," Rachael said, scowling at Shaw. "I suggest that we don't do anything for the moment. The important thing is that you are all right." She faced Sarah and rubbed her shoulders.

"Are you all right?" Jack asked again, sounding worried.

"Yes," she said quickly. "I am fine. Well, I am better than I was before. I mean, I will be all right." She was shaking and gave a fake smile. "Right now, you have to go before my dad comes."

Shaw said something that would have earned him detention if he said it in class as he jumped to his feet and ran toward the door.

"Wait here!" Sarah yelled. She reached out with her hand, holding the broken amulet pieces. "Everyone take a part." Jack and Shaw went to grasp theirs, but Rachael grabbed their hands, preventing them.

"Don't," Rachael ordered. "Why should we? Why did he want to take these? We don't know anything about this thing."

Sarah faltered for a moment. She felt stupid for an instant with her hand outstretched. The amulet felt very heavy under Rachael's stair.

"Oh, for crying out loud!" Shaw blurted. "What would it hurt, Rach? Chill." He pushed past her and grabbed the upper left side piece. Jack got to the upper right, and seeing Rachael standing looking worried, he took the other piece and put it in Rachael's hand.

"Let's go before we are caught," Jack called out, looking out the front room window. He pushed Rachael out the door.

"We could all be making the biggest mistakes," Rachael gasped.

Seeing no car coming, Shaw hurried to the sidewalk, seemed to slow down, and walked smoothly. Rachael kept blurting unfinished questions all the way out before Jack hurried her out the door.

"We each need to sort this out on our own, just as we said before!" He huffed, pushing and pulling her.

Sarah shut the door behind them. She turned her amulet piece in her hand, examining it as its light faded. Noticing that she was right on the other side of the door again, she moved away as if it were on fire. She shivered and felt very cold, placing her part of the Telum Deos in her pocket. Rubbing her arms, she started to walk even though she didn't know where to go. Lights flashed through the window, telling her father was home.

"What do I do?" she said out loud, moving left and right. She went back and forth until she saw the fridge. Bolting for it, she hit her ankle on the way past her table. Letting out a shriek that sounded like running over a gerbil, she tottered to the fridge and stuck her head in it.

"Hello," her father said as soon as he opened the door.

"Hey, Dad." She sounded too enthusiastic from inside the fridge.

"How was your day? I'm sorry that I was called away."

"Fine."

"Did Miss Amanda give you a ride home?"

"Yep." *Why did she sound so fake?* she asked herself as she rolled her eyes.

"Uh, dear, what you look'n for?" her father asked behind her.

"Food."

"What have you been doing since you been home?"

"She forced her way up to see me," her grandfather called behind her.

"No, I didn't!" She yelled. Pain erupted from the side of her head. She shot up so quickly that she hit the cooling tray above her left ear. "Awe, man… No, I didn't. You tricked me up there." She held her head and closed her eyes against the pain.

"Did you hurt the fridge?" Her dad said dully.

"David," Renfield pleaded, coming down the stairs. "On all the lives of all the mice, rats, and spiders I have eaten this past week, she broke in upstairs and forced me to talk to her."

"How can you lie like that?" She argued.

"I kept my word," Renfield was now next to her father, who turned his back to him and looked up to the ceiling.

"Dad, why would I do that?"

"Enough!" Her father yelled, slamming his briefcase on the counter. "I never told Sarah what was going on because I know what you both would be like together."

He took deep breaths and fixed his glasses. "Now the question is, what are we going to do to keep this a secret?"

"What secret?" Renfield asked.

"This family's secret," David cried. He seemed to go from stages of being relaxed to bursting out. "Everything in this family is secret. I did my best to keep Sarah out of all this stuff so we could have a happy, normal life. Now that she knows, we must ensure it stays between the three of us."

Sarah gave her grandfather a frightening look. He responded by shaking his head quickly, telling her not to say anything. David ran a hand through his hair, endeavoring to calm down.

"I want us all to agree that it goes no further." David looked at his father and then at Sarah.

"I promise not to tell anyone else," Renfield said. He went to cross his heart but stopped halfway, looking disgusted at the mistake he almost made.

Sarah opened her mouth to explain that her friends knew as well, but to her horror, all that came out was, "I promise." Her lips moved, and she said that three of her friends knew. She grabbed her throat and tried to say anything, but nothing came out.

"Good," her father said. "Now that is done. I think it best to go on with our lives as best we can. I need to go to bed. I'm drained. We will go over rules, boundaries, actions, and responsibilities later."

Sarah opened her mouth to speak again, but nothing came out again. With one hand on her throat, she banged the fridge with the other, striving to get her father's attention. Her father had just started walking up the stairs. He didn't even raise his tired head but said, "Dear please be careful and stop banging into things. I have a headache."

Sarah's arms fell in shock at what just happened as her grandfather patted his son on the back as he passed. She gave him a dirty look, raising her shoulders and motioning why he was not allowing her to speak. With his free hand that was not leading her father to his room, he waved it at her. She was free to talk but couldn't move her feet just as both disappeared from her view.

"Seriously?" She cried.

"Dear, please," her father called back to her.

Sarah groaned in frustration, folding her arms. She tried to jump, but her legs wouldn't budge. It was as if they were made of wood. She strived to swing her weight to lift her left leg and swing in front of her. Her legs were dead and stiff, but moved with only her hips directing them. She steadied herself with her hands on the counters. Almost toppling over, she swung her right leg. She moved, feeling very stupid, muttering under her breath. She had moved out of the kitchen and was running out of the counter to steady herself. Reaching for the nearest chair in the dining room was difficult as it was just about three inches too far away.

Unexpectedly, she started to fall forward. She screamed and was scared by the horrible feeling of not being able to use her lower half. She reached out to brace herself but froze again before hitting the floor. She floated inches above the ground.

"Quite please!" her father called from upstairs again as she offered an angry look up the stairs. "I don't ask for much, but please quit it down tonight!" She twisted and tried to free her arms and legs, but couldn't. She began to rise and saw her grandfather standing at the top of the stairs, waving his hand and motioning for her to stand up.

"Really," she folded her arms again, "being controlled like this is intolerable," she said tersely.

"I had but little choice," Renfield said, taking a quick look down the hall where he had left her father. "If I hadn't done it, you would have told your father everything."

"Yeah," she spat back.

"I have known your father longer than you; if you had, he would have…"

Sarah still gave Renfield an obstinate look as he hurried down the stairs. She would look at him and then at her legs.

"Oh, my apologies," and she was free with a wave of his hand.

She groaned and massaged her legs. "I don't appreciate having parts of me turned into Barbie Doll plastic."

"Sshh, keep your voice down. We don't want him to be grumpy any more than he already is. Especially when he learns that the seminar that he was called to be an emergency speaker tonight was controlled by me."

Her anger seemed to change in an instant to surprise. "You did what?"

"Sshhh!" He urged her again, holding a finger to his lips. "All I did was call up some guy at the university on the other side of town and hypnotize him into filling a room full of people. I had him call David and say their key speaker was taken ill and they needed him. Just before he arrived, I had this fool put me on speaker, and I hypnotized the audience. Please don't give me that look. It wasn't as bad as all that. I gave him a standing ovation for the words he driveled off."

"Why did you do that? How did you do that?" Sarah said, almost laughing.

"I wanted to talk to you, but I had to tell you when the amulet lit up. But please, we have bigger things to tend to, dear." Renfield came close to her and held her shoulders. "I know we have never been given the opportunity to learn of one another, but I wish for that to change. Trust me, it is better for now. Please give me this opportunity to earn your trust. Play along with your father for now and give him his elution for as long as possible. He can barely grasp what it means that you know the truth about me and your situation. Imagine how hard it would be for him to understand that your friends, strangers to him, have now joined us?"

Sarah eyed him thoughtfully. "No more paralyzing or voiceovers?" she said hotly.

"I will only do it if the situation merits it," he said warmly. From the look she gave him, he said quickly, "There might be a time when you will want to do a Winona Ryder and sing 'Jump In The Line.' I wager I might have you doing it better than she did."

"Who?"

"Winona Ryder?" He protested. "From Beetlejuice, come on. Hasn't your father instructed you in the classics? This from a gentleman who claims to teach history. Forgive me, I have been stuck in a room where I only had television."

"All right," she spat, smirking. His face and mannerisms were so odd. It filled her with a refreshing warmth. "I will trust you for tonight, but we will see what happens tomorrow."

"Agreed." He smiled, nodding his head vigorously.

"I can't imagine it getting any weirder than this one."

"Oh, my dear," his voice was somber and serious. "With these two worlds coming together, the order of the day is strange."

CHAPTER NINE

HARD TIMES BRING OUT WHO IS THERE FOR YOU

Her alarm sounded in her ears like hammers, and it felt like she hadn't slept at all. She had eaten last night and went straight to bed. She slept well, but all the strain was catching up to her. She got up and stretched, wishing this Friday would just be over.

"What if I just stayed in bed today?" she said, falling and burying her face in her pillow. Then she could hear her father, "Sarah, hurry or you will be late for school!" she said, mocking her father's voice. "Why is it a requirement for teachers to have annoying voices?"

She hurried and got ready as quickly as possible. She was downstairs and eating a piece of toast even before her father came down.

"Well, this is a welcome sight," her father stated, smiling proudly. "What brought this change on?"

"T.G.I.F., Dad," she said, taking another bite.

"I am glad you are up. I wanted to talk to you about everything going on."

"Wait, Dad. I just need a second. I just remembered something," she said nervously.

"This is important," he protested.

She ran up the stairs, "I just need to get something. Won't be but a sec."

She ran into her room and removed the pants she had worn the previous day from her clothing hamper. Her piece of the amulet was still in her pocket. She almost wished that it wasn't there. Shaking her head, she put it in her pocket, put the last piece of toast in her mouth, and went to leave. She was about to shut the door when she suddenly felt someone watching her. There was nothing in the hall. There was nothing in her room as she looked around. The trees outside were moving slightly in the breeze, but there was no sign of anything. She walked down the stairs a little slower, unable to get rid of that feeling.

"I wanted to put the thought to you if we go away this weekend." Her dad asked, sitting down to a bowl of cereal.

"I have a game tonight."

"I am aware of that, but our family is more important than one game."

"Our family?" She sounded angrier than she was, but didn't like where this was going.

"Yes, you and I," he said, finishing a mouthful. "Our family."

"What about grandpa? Isn't he part of the family?"

Her father hurried, finished what was in his mouth, and set his spoon down in its bowl. "Yes, he is a member of this family, but you can guess why we can't live like most people."

"Yes, I can guess that, but I don't want a lecture right now."

"This is not a lecture." He didn't sound angry, but she could tell he was serious.

"Then what is it?"

"It's a discussion," he folded his hands, placing his elbows on the table. "We just can't go on like nothing happened. We need to act that way, but like it or not, things have changed.

"A discussion?" she said, slipping her shoes on and standing next to the door. "A discussion is why people eat good cereal when they are younger, but when they get older, they grab boxes that don't have a cartoon animal on them. They grab one that says bran on it and looks like it should be served in a rest home."

"Yes, that is a discussion, but that is not important at this time." He leaned back.

"I really don't want to discuss what keeps you regular, but can't we just go today and not do this?"

Her dad rubbed his hands through his hair in frustration.

"Dad, don't ever play poker. You always run your hand through what hair you have left when you are angry."

"I AM NOT ANGRY!" He yelled, slamming his hands down on the table. It would have been terrible, but one hand hit the back end of his spoon, causing milk and cereal to be catapulted across the room. Sarah let out a small squeak of a scream.

Composing himself quickly and placing his hands under the table, he added, "And I'm not losing my hair."

"Ok, Dad," she said softly, rolling her eyes sarcastically down to the floor.

The clock ticking was all they had to pass the silence they had given each other.

"We will leave tonight and spend some time away from all this." Her father said briskly.

"Yes, Dad." She sounded so dull.

He got up and took his bowl to the sink. "I know you are having a harder time than you should, but I am trying."

"Yes, Dad."

"All right," he sounded happier. "Let's have a better day. I am sorry for my anger. I need to clean this up, and I will meet you in the car. We will make this a good day. Please think about what you want to do tonight and tomorrow, hmm?"

"Yes, Dad."

"All right," he said happily, taking a towel and walking back to the table. "Will you say anything else other than yes, Dad?"

She walked to the door and removed the car key, unlocking its door. "Dad, I am sorry for what I said."

"Thank you."

"I don't know what lens you are looking through, but every time you go to the barber, he has to spend less and less time on your roof."

"You get out of here." He said playfully, throwing the towel at her, laughing.

They drove to school in better spirits and enjoyed the radio together. They didn't say much but didn't have to. The school day was almost the same as usual, as Sarah had mixed feelings about lunchtime. Her anxiety began to overpower her as the bell for lunch was about to sound. With it came the rush of class like horses out of a starter's gate. She was one of the first in line for lunch, and after getting her food, she sat in her usual spot.

"Sarah." Rachael came and sat opposite her. "Has there been anything new?"

"No, unless you want me to talk about how they expect us to eat this." She groaned. "Since when did everything become health food without flavor?"

"Thank what everyone calls the former first lady. That's the last lady in line for her lunch." Rachael leaned forward over her tray. "Do you have it?"

"Have what?"

She bent even lower, looking around. "Do you have IT?"

"Have what, Pepto Bismol, for this?" She pointed her fork at her tray. "There isn't enough Alka-Seltzer for this menu."

"Not that!" Rachael whispered urgently. "What you gave us last night."

"Oh, the amulet," Sarah said, leaning back. "Yeah, I have it in my pock…"

"Will you keep quiet!?" Rachael spat, looking around again quickly.

"If I were you, I wouldn't worry about that so much," Sarah said, taking a mouthful.

"How can you say that?"

"You failed to notice what you just dipped into your food."

"OH, dear duck dynasty," Rachael cried, looking down at her chest, which now had spots of food on her blouse. She grabbed her napkin and rubbed her chest frantically. "This is going to stain!"

"Hey," Sarah bellowed as someone bumped her from behind.

"Sorry," a boy said. Sarah looked up to see that it was Perry. She knew nothing about him besides his name and that he was one of the cutest and most popular boys in school. His eyes were fixed on what Rachael was doing.

"It's all right," Sarah said. She felt horrified and wished she were wearing something better than what she had on, or that her hair was.

"Move along," Rachael ordered. "Sarah, I must use my emergency cleaning kit from my locker. I will be back in a moment."

"All right." Sarah watched her friend go and wondered if she had something in her teeth. She felt her teeth with her tongue. Something might be there as she picked up her spoon and turned it around to see her reflection. Her distorted appearance showed back at her as she raised her upper lip, and she thought she saw a nose hair.

"I didn't mean to have your friend leave," said the same voice that came from behind her, this time in front of her.

She shut her eyes and said softly, "Oh please, no more."

"Sorry?" he asked, sitting across from her with his lunch tray.

"Uh, this spoon is dirty and must have fallen on the floor," she said quickly. It was then that her curse started to show. Only Rachael knew about what they called her curse. Whenever Sarah was around a boy she liked, her speech would triple in speed.

"You're Sarah, right?" he asked, adjusting how he sat on his bench.

"Yeah, Sarah, that's me. You know me…. Sarah?"

"Isn't that your name, and I don't really know you? That's why I'm asking." He lowered his eyebrows.

"*WHY*!?!" she screamed in her head. "*What was going on in his head? His hairstyle complemented his eyes. Those eyes possibly were dripping with loyalty, confidence, honesty, and passion.*"

"Well, I heard you were the daughter of Mr. Fields. He's a good teacher." It was so nice to have him say something to break in on her lost thoughts.

"Yes, he is my mad, uh, dad, my dad, he is dad, my dad. Father, that's it." She added with a laugh.

"*Why did the laugh sound like a chipmunk?*" she quivered with the thought.

"It is hard to have a parent as a teacher. My dad is Mr. Holmwood. I know kids don't like him so much, but he isn't that bad."

"Yeah, not bad…"

She put her elbow on the table and raised her chin in her hands. He looked at her oddly before someone from the side of the table cleared their throat.

"Perry, can I have my seat?" Jack asked.

"Sure," Perry said, standing up and getting his lunch tray. "I was just leaving. Good to meet you, aaahh, Sarah." He walked away.

"What are you doing talking to a guy like Perry?" Jack asked, sitting down hard. "He doesn't come down to sit with us. And what is up with your food?"

"What about it?"

"You put your elbow in your potatoes."

"Oh, dear Detroit Democrats!"

"You sound like Rachael," Jack said, shaking his head.

Sarah shook off and wiped away what she could from her elbow. She rolled her eyes up in her head and felt like she would cry. Perry saw everything. How senseless could she be? Shaw sat down and immediately started eating quickly.

"What's the rush?" Jack asked, looking at Shaw.

"I don't want to miss anything new in the world of weirdness," he said with a mouth full.

Jack made a face like he was going to be sick. Luckily, Rachael returned, sitting next to Sarah. Her shirt looked almost brand new.

"Did you change your shirt?" Sarah asked.

"I had to," she said, straightening her tray. "I will have to do extensive work tonight to save it. I can't stand being seen with a stai…" She saw Sarah's elbow, got up, and sat on her other side, further away from the stained elbow.

Shaw let out a large belch that turned the heads of other students from nearby tables. Jack, Rachael, and Sarah were used to this.

"What's new?" Shaw asked, raising a napkin to his lips, acting like a king. He raised his hand and rotated it slightly as a prince waving to commoners. The other table occupants turned away. "What's the latest?" Shaw asked again, eagerly changing from royalty to a child leaning forward in his seat.

Sarah started, "Well, Rachael stained her clothes, and Perry came over…"

"You know what I mean." Shaw cut her off.

"Why was Perry over here anyway?" Jack sounded angry. "That guy couldn't even remember your name. He probably would have a heart attack if you took away his blankie and asked him if his diapers were pull-ups, idiot."

"Ok, that's enough," Sarah said, holding her hands up. "I think we need to all chill."

"Chill?" Jack said, questioning her. "You want all of us to chill with all this going on?"

"Yes, I can do it. So why can't you?" Sarah straightened her back and took a long drink.

"How could you chill when you had that smudge of potatoes on your chin and that piece of corn between your teeth when Perry was here?" Jack said smartly.

"Oh, fudge nuggets, really?" Sarah barked and felt her teeth with her finger.

Jack and Shaw broke out laughing. "You don't have anything of the sort," Rachael said, saving her. She gave the boys a harsh look. "I think you are cruel."

"Yeah, but it's fun," Jack said, hitting Shaw's knuckles in a fist bump.

"Ok, ok," Sarah said, coming to herself. "Let's go on with our lives. Nothing is new, and I think we should act normally. Or as normal as possible for what we call ordinary." Sarah was looking at Shaw, mixing his milk with corn and eating them together quickly.

"Well, what are we going to do?" Rachael asked, lowering her voice. "I didn't sleep a wink last night, wondering what we are going to do with these, these things." She was padding her pocket.

"We will go around doing what we always did," Sarah said, sounding as if she were a teacher.

"Sarah is right," Jack added quickly. "What would our parents do if they found out? My mom would freak, and others wouldn't believe us. What else can we do?"

No one spoke for a moment, and all they heard was Shaw sipping his food. "We will just take it a day at a time." Sarah nodded.

"All right, are you guys going to the game tonight?" Shaw sounded disappointed that his life would not be added to the supernatural that day.

"I don't know," Sarah groaned. "My dad needs a moment."

"Yeah," all three of her friends said together.

"Parents," Shaw squealed. "Can't live with them and wish you could be here without them."

"Well, see you all if you are there, and good luck, Sarah," Rachael said, taking her tray and standing up.

Shaw followed her, eating off his tray as he walked. Jack didn't say anything and seemed to eat slower. Jack got up without a word and joined the other finished kids. It felt strange to be alone, so she got up and took care of her tray. She walked more leisurely than average to her locker.

Classes went on just as they always did, as she finished practice after school. It was not very pleasant for her when she went to tell her coach that she didn't know if she would be there that night, but luckily, her father had already told her. Her coach still didn't look happy, though. She waited for her dad next to their car just like usual, and it felt like it was almost a typical day.

"So, where would you like to go?" He asked happily.

"Home?" she said, shrugging her shoulders.

"No, this weekend," he laughed, getting into their car.

"Oh, I don't know. I forgot."

They drove on, going over some different destinations and activities. They couldn't agree on anything, and it became heated when it came to the game. "They need me." Sarah spat.

"They will be fine." Her father reassured her.

They kept going until they pulled up in their driveway. "Dad, if I don't play, they will lose." She shouted, going in the door.

"Why do you always talk, teen, when you are angry with me? All the way over here."

"I think she should go." Her grandfather said, surprisingly, as soon as the door shut.

"Dad, what are you doing out of your room?" Her father shouted, checking the door was shut and the windows closed.

"I think she should go to the game."

"Thanks, Grandpa," Sarah said, folding her arms again after dropping her bag on the table.

"No, I think things are too hot now." Her father was shaking his head. "We all just need to calm down, and you should go back to your room."

"I need to get out again. The sun will be down by the time the game is on, and I want to see her play."

"Absolutely not!" Her father shouted. He threw his briefcase down and went to nudge Renfield to the stairs. When he went to push him, it was as if he were striving to move a brick wall.

"If you let me go. I will not bother you for a month." Renfield started quickly.

"He can't go!" Sarah cried.

"Oh, I can't. You don't know me!" Renfield sounded even more like a teenager than she did.

"You can't go looking like that," Sarah said, shaking her head.

"You are not going!"

Renfield held up a hand in front of his son's face. "If you let me go, I will give you one month of peace, and I swear I will do something for Sarah that will make it worth her while. I will disguise myself so well, even you won't recognize me."

Her father seemed to walk back and forth, thinking about this repeatedly. "A month?" he asked, tapping his toes impatiently.

"I promise, one month," Renfield stated, sounding knowledgeable.

"You won't do anything for Sarah, like make her win?" her father added.

"How could you think such a thing?" Her grandfather acted like he was outraged at the very thought.

Her father's pace quickened. He turned to her as if to say something, then turned away to think some more. He leaned over the kitchen counter momentarily and turned to speak again.

"Can I play?" she asked before he could say anything.

"That's a yes!" Renfield shouted excitedly. "Whoa!" He screeched and turned into a bat, flying upstairs quickly, even though David never said anything.

Sarah was stunned and waited for her father to stop shaking his head. Once he had finished, all he said was, "You get used to it." David rolled his eyes and added, "Oh, I have your phone. Some rather large kid had it in the office. You wouldn't believe what it took to have him give it up. Please put it in your sports bag. Keep it off till after the game."

She did her homework and got ready for her game. They drove back to their school as if it were supposed to happen. Sarah couldn't help but look around and search for what was strange. She couldn't see anything other than the dogs in the neighborhood, who seemed to be barking more than they typically did. He followed her to the locker room, this time without a word. He, too, was looking around at other people a little longer than he would typically have.

"Good luck and try not to think of anything else than the game." He said, hugging her. "It's just another game, all right?"

"Yeah, Dad," she said, forcing a smile.

She changed and warmed up on the court. She didn't do as well as usual and couldn't help but keep looking up at the crowd gathering in the stands. There was a little old woman who kept looking at her every time she shot. Was that him? Could he do that? Was he there?

"Sarah, you're starting guard." From behind her, the coach said before the buzzer sounded that warmup time was over. As she went to her seat, she searched the stands and saw Rachael sitting between Jack and Shaw. They waved to her when they noticed their eyes meeting.

For the first half, she was doing horribly. She couldn't clear her head, missed three shots, and blew two passes. She was benched for the second quarter when the ball was thrown in, and the crowd seemed to quiet down.

It was almost halftime with under two minutes to go. All the scoreboard told her was that it was hopeless. With most of her team that was on the bench looking down, they didn't notice one of the school faculty members rushing into the gym and onto the court toward the head referee. Every whistle blew as every player, referee, coach, and even ball boy was angered at this terrible breach of game protocol. The faculty member was shouting and pointing to the main door she had just come through, but only the referee she was speaking to could hear her. Whatever she was saying, it was making her jump up and down in excitement.

The referee patted her on the hand and blew the whistle, stopping the clock as he waved his arms, stopping the game. His fellow line refs ran after him in confusion as they bolted to the announcing booth at the top of the stands.

"What's up?" Sarah's fellow player, who was sitting next to her, asked.

Sarah shrugged, "Don't know."

Everyone's attention was drawn to them until a panting voice of excitement sounded over the microphone. "Ladies and gentlemen, we must pause the match for a moment for an, well, an unbelievable announcement."

It was then that several people who appeared to be private security began to enter the gym and line up toward the closest seat on the stands. Several of them sat in a square, moving people over to where one or two people could sit, being surrounded by them.

"Everyone," the announcer shouted, making the microphone squawk from feedback. Please welcome an amazing, special guest to our school, city, and game: Mr. Abel Makkonen Tesfaye, better known as The Weeknd."

Even the player on the opposite team, holding the ball in frustration, dropped it along with everyone's jaws.

"NO!?!" Sarah said to herself.

Abel waved to everyone and shook every hand as he passed them as he made his way, greeting the players with members of the security guards flanking him. He was full of energy as he waved to everyone. As he passed Sarah, he gave a wink and thumbs up. Her teammates shrieked in surprise as Abel kissed her forehead and finished with the other players before taking the seat his security made for him. Sarah lowered her head to her knees.

The refineries returned and strived to start the game again, but it wasn't useless. Everyone in the audience and team couldn't do anything now that he was there. No one had even scored since he arrived; there were only two completed passes, as players' eyes were on him, not the game. It was a relief when the halftime buzzer rang.

Sarah was the only one who got up with her focus on the locker room for halftime. She was convinced that her grandfather had somehow disguised himself as Abel, and this was all a farce. She was the only one doing what she was supposed to when the announcer's voice changed to the referee once more.

"Attention, please attention," he said, sounding like he was crying. "With all due respect to our band and regular halftime show, we have another special guest who will be joining us soon for a surprise special treat for a halftime show provided for you by Mr. Fields, our history teacher and our own number 12, Sarah Fields."

"Oh No!" She cried as she felt all the blood drain from her body.

"Friends, I can't believe I have been asked to announce that The Weeknd will be performing 'Save Your Tears' with a surprise guest, so please take your seats as we will be extending the halftime for this unbelievable performance."

No one heard the rest of what the announcement had after he said the title of the song, as the entire stadium erupted. Mr. Tesfaye got up, waving and smiling.

"I don't believe it," she moaned as she was almost stampeded back to the bench where she sat.

There weren't words for the elation everyone felt. Even the single person bringing the microphone for Abel wouldn't let go of it as Abel held it. It took a security member a full minute to force the child to let it go so Abel could test the microphone and ask for silence.

"He wouldn't do this," Sarah shouted as his back began to hurt from all the students hitting it, slapping, and hugging her.

As the music began, there were shouts and yells of approval that the school had never known. Something in the music seemed to turn a switch in her, and she was instantly happy. It wasn't even to the third note when she was caught up in the moment and felt instantly happier than she could ever remember.

The Weeknd began to sing right at her, "I saw you dancing in a crowded room." At that moment, everything she doubted was gone, as it occurred to her that this really was Abel Tesfaye.

The music continued as Abel slowly moved when he raised his hand to his ear to have the audience join him after he sang the part, "save your ears for another."

Everyone sang, "save your tears for another day," with the music playing, and he had them sing it again, "save your tears for another day."

With every eye on him, Able danced smoothly and pointed to the door he came in. It seemed the entire city exploded with cheers as the school's second special guest came in, and when she did, Sarah was positively milled with people's uncontrollable excitement.

Ariana Grande came in singing her part, "met you once under a Pisces moon."

The roar was deafening as Able, in his suite, and Ariana, in the most beautiful dress in the world, danced around each other gracefully. Several of their guards came and circled them when others motioned for both team players to dance on the court. It started with Sarah, as her fellow players pushed her forward.

One guard took her by the hand and danced with her, with The Weeknd and Ariana Grande singing in the center of the court.

It was pure elation as Sarah just danced, feeling the music more than hearing it. She floated on the floor as she saw tears of joy in her teammates, as some of their opponents couldn't stop shaking from the thrill. She wished that this moment would never stop.

The song ended with Abel and Ariana embracing and shouting for approval from all. Sarah's hand hurt from clapping so hard, and her cheeks hurt from smiling so stiffly. The audience cheered louder as Abel waved to them, all circling.

Ariana shouted, "The Weeknd!" clapping herself for him.

"Ariana Grande," Abel reciprocated, bowing to her in respect.

Abel waved for people to quiet down as security started to lead players back to their seats, however, Sarah's large guard gently held her shoulder firm, keeping her in place on the court.

It took several pleads from The Weeknd to have people quite down when he stated, "what a privilege to be here tonight!" Another couple of minutes for the crowed to be calmed after this statement.

Able continued, "I wish to thank all of you for this opportunity. It was just like magic that Ariana and I were able to be here tonight as everything worked out perfectly for us to be here this evening.

The roar was earsplitting for a moment. It was Ariana who asked for silence before she said, smiling, "and a special thanks to Lon Chaney Jr. High for having us!"

Even the other school fans and team cheered with applause, whistles, and shouts of approval. The court was clear save for The Weeknd, Ariana, guards, and Sarah.

"But before we go, we would like to thank a very special person," Ariana said, holding a hand toward Sarah. The guard who danced with Sarah turned his dark glasses from her to the center of the court. The other guards parted as Sarah's legs turned to jelly. He was leading her to be with them. When she entered the circle of safety, Ariana gave her the sweetest hug, and then Abel followed.

"Thank you, Sarah, for allowing us to join you this evening and sing to you," Abel said, smiling, "and thank you once more, Ariana." They bowed together, smiling as the audience cheered. Both singers handed the microphones to a guard, and each leaned over to Sarah.

"Seriously," Abel said, "thank you, Sarah. It was a pleasure to meet you." Before he gave her another quick hug. After letting her go, he reached up, removed his necktie, and handed it to her. Ariana also hugged Sarah again, "god bless and best wishes," she said so only Sarah could hear. Then she removed her earrings and held up Sarah's dumb struck hand and put them in it.

The security guard who had danced with Sarah grunted, "A photo, please?"

"Of course," both Abel and Ariana said, smiling together. Sarah suddenly panicked. Her phone! Where was her phone? All the enjoyment and excitement she had seemed to focus on a single cell phone, the guard removed it from his pocket. It was her phone.

All of a sudden, with a few clicks, the pictures were done. Both singers were waving their way out, and the single guard who had her phone handed it back to her and, for the first time, smiled.

"Thank you for dancing with your grandfather," he smiled as a tear fell from his cheek.

Sarah couldn't believe it. It was him all along. Someone was saying something over the intercom. All the fame had left the school, but the excitement couldn't be stronger.

"How do you know them?!" Kris yelled, shaking Sarah by the shoulders. Everyone on the floor mobbed Sarah. At first, she thought she was in trouble with everyone trying to reach her. She began to relax and understood it was admiration they were giving.

"Please return to your seats and let the game continue after halftime, " the announcer said.

Sarah couldn't stop smiling from all the handshakes and back slaps. Even Kris wouldn't let her go because she was much bigger and the best center they had. It would have been difficult even if she tried to get away.

"I knew I could dance, but I didn't know I could inspire everyone to follow me so well," Kris said, sighing with pleasure. There was no end to the fun from everyone and comments of excitement.

The rest of the game was amazing as her team came back from their biggest deficit and won. Sarah couldn't miss, as each moment was heaven. Even with the loss, the other players didn't seem to care. As the buzzer rang, no one cared for who had the last shot. Everyone, player and audience member alike, rushed and carried Sarah in approval.

"Fun is over. Time to keep the game going," their coach ordered, struggling to herd her players back to the locker room and keep others out.

"Hey, coach," another player called as they walked to the locker room. "Save your tears for another day, and let us keep tonight."

"Shut it, Haskie!" She shouted back. "We have another game to get ready for next week.

Sarah couldn't stop laughing or smiling. She would never forget this or ever wanted to.

Chapter Ten

Someone Call Pest Control

The team joked that their coach's mother died in childbirth. Not because their coach was so evil at times and it took a life to bring something so wicked in this world, but because she gave birth to twins, their coach, and a basketball.

"Focus," their coach pleaded, "what's all the fuss anyway over two people who can sing. Probably the first time on the court anyway.

Jessie yelled to her, "Gee, coach, don't you like anyone famous?"

The coach laughed. "Ha, the only one who came close was Tom Hanks." The only problem was that he fell in love with the volleyball on that island when it should have been a basketball.

"No, coach," Jessie called back while everyone else laughed, "that's just wrong."

"If you are going to fall in love with a ball, it should be a basketball, not some volleyball." Their coach seemed unimpressed with The Weeknd and Ariana on that basis.

"Just Google their music." Was the last thing they said to her as Sarah was allowed to leave the locker room? She was mobbed with a hallway full of people waiting for her. She shook hands, bumped knuckles, and gave high-fives.

She found her father waiting for her next to their car. "We won! Dad, sorry I'm late, they just wouldn't let me go. What a night, how did Grandpa do that?"

"Dad," she added as he said nothing but just stared at her.

"Get in," he ordered angrily.

"What," she asked, not understanding.

"GET IN NOW!" he yelled.

She jumped and suddenly felt her euphoria being pushed aside with fear. Her hands shook as she opened the door and got in the car. Her father sped out of the parking lot, not waiting for her to put on her seatbelt. She didn't know why, but tears began to form in the corner of her eyes. Her father gripped the steering wheel so hard that she was surprised it didn't break as he drove faster than Miss Amanda.

"Did you know?" Her father shouted.

"Know what, Dad?" She sniveled.

"Did you know he was going to do that stupid stunt?" he asked, taking a corner very fast, forcing her to lean on her door.

"Dad, you are scaring me."

"Good!" he yelled.

"What's wrong with what he did?"

"Really?" he shouted. "You don't see the harm in what he just pulled. What will happen when people learn The Weeknd and Ariana Grande were mystically rerouted to meet and sing at our school? What do you think their managers are going to do? What will happen when they figure out what really happened? What will happen if they start asking how things worked out to get them there? We can't be part of people's lives like this."

She did her best to keep more tears from coming as her father slowed down to the speed limit. He was still breathing hard, and guilt was creeping up her throat.

"I didn't think dad. I'm sor..."

"You're sorry," he spat back. "Sorry, sorry, I just want to know what we will do?"

They kept driving on until they turned down their road. To Sarah's horror, her father pulled the car over, still several houses down from theirs. He turned the engine off, and they just sat there with their heads down.

"I'm sorry," he said, breaking the silence.

"It's not your fault. You don't know what he can be like. It's my fault. I don't know what we are going to do."

They both shared the moment when Sarah felt so different from how she had felt before. Her insides twisted and turned as if her stomach were on a rubber band being pulled by her heartbeat. She reached over and held her father's hand. As soon as she did, he started to cry and squeezed it hard. He was balling even more than she was.

"I just don't want to move you again, and we have to stay here and fight whatever is coming. I don't know if I can do it." Her dad whimpered.

"Dad," she said softly. "We will do it together." She didn't know where her strength came from when she said it.

He nodded vigorously and wiped his tears away with the palms of his hands.

"Thank you," he said, struggling to sound normal again. "I love you."

"I love you too, Dad," she said vehemently. After letting go of his hand, she added, "Now, save your tears…"

"Oh, that's not going away anytime soon, right?"

"NO, it's not!"

They started to laugh for a moment, and Sarah was feeling better. "What if we order pizza tonight and watch a movie with Grandpa?" he asked, reaching to start the car.

"Sure," she said, smiling, enjoying the little light of happiness that had returned to them.

"I sometimes sneak up and watch with him and…"

"What is it?" she asked. "The car won't start." He exclaimed, trying again and again, but the car wouldn't do anything. Suddenly, there was a bright flash from under the hood, a sharp squeak, and a horrible smell filled the car with whisps of smoke from the engine.

"What was that?" She inquired, holding her nose.

"Wait here," her dad said, popping the hood. "I first thought I pushed the engine too hard before, but this is new," he said, getting out.

He shut the door behind him and opened the hood. As he did this, Sarah pulled out her phone and turned it back on. As it powered on, she saw the top of her father's head and his hand waving some of the smoke away.

"Sarah, get out of the car!" he ordered.

"What is it?"

"Get out!"

"Get in, get out," she mocked, thinking this was a joke. She set her phone down and moved around the car next to her dad.

"What is it, ah!" she squealed. The light from the hood showed the power lines from the battery had been severed. Right next to them was a two-foot-long rat scorched and burned. Then she breathed in the smell and held her nose.

"How did that thing get in there?"

Her father didn't answer. He wasn't even looking at it, but was searching around the area. She strained her ears to hear. It sounded like a typical night, but it still sounded like more dogs were barking than usual.

"Grab your stuff." Her father ordered, sounding scared. She didn't wait but hurried and grabbed her phone from the car and her sports bag. As soon as she did, she faltered momentarily, looking at the bag with her clothes in it.

"We need to move." Her father called.

She took her phone with one hand and, with the other, grabbed her bag and flung it over her shoulder. Her father had thrown the rat into some bushes by the tail and shut the hood. Her phone began to ding, telling her that she had messages. She stuffed it into her bag and took out her amulet piece. She held it and took her father's hand with the other. He pulled her along, searching with his eyes all over for anything. She moved right with him, wishing her legs weren't sore from the game.

They ran toward their house, which they could see in the distance. "Why are you so worried?" Sarah puffed.

"It may be nothing," he gasped. "I need to do more cardio, ah."

Their running became a jog until they reached their driveway. Sarah's father slowed to a pace and kept searching all around them.

"Go inside, Sarah. I'll be in a moment."

Sarah didn't say anything but opened the door, watched her father remove something from his pocket, and started to empty its contents until he reached the door. As she watched from the open door, Sarah thought it looked like a salt shaker. Once inside, her father pushed Sarah softly against the wall and shut the door. He watched through their window, patting Sarah reassuringly on the shoulder.

"I think it will be all right." He said, bending over, still panting.

Then they heard something like tiny claws scratching across the room above them. They both froze as they looked up, following the noise crossing the ceiling. Then there were more.

"Must be at least three up there," her father whispered, still breathing fast.

"What are they? Is it Grandpa?" she asked.

"No," her father mouthed, holding a finger to his lips while he tiptoed to the table.

Sarah pushed herself against the wall by the door. Fear seemed to be growing from within her. She felt cold as her home didn't seem safe anymore. She never noticed so many dark spots where things could be hiding.

More scratching noises came from upstairs. Her father held a hand to tell Sarah to stay put. He reached for the light switch, but with a failed click, nothing happened.

"They chewed through the power somewhere," he said lowly. He then leaned over next to the kitchen table as if he were feeling for something under it, still looking up.

Sarah let out a small squeak of a scream when the skittering of claws came from the living room to her right.

"Dad?" Sarah whimpered.

"Stay calm and stay put." He barked, still feeling under the table for something.

Sarah heard more scratching, which sounded like it was coming from her room, the hall, and the stairs. She followed the noise in the dark, and then, from the streetlamp light through their kitchen window, she saw it. Two tiny eyes reflected like mirrors the head of a giant rat. It sniffed the air next to the first wooden spindle banister from the hallway.

"Dad?" Sarah cried, sobbing softly, dropping everything in her hands to hold her face in fear.

Two soft clicks sounded under the table as her father straightened, holding a short sword. He held it defensively, taking small, quiet steps toward Sarah, facing the rat. The rodent moved down two more steps in a flash before pausing to sniff the air. Sarah saw in the dim light its whiskers, twitching, searching, smelling the atmosphere, shimmering in the soft light. It moved quickly down the stairs, taking two or three at a time before freezing for a moment. More scratching came from above them, causing them to look up. Then, more from the living room. They were all around them.

Wham! "Sarah, get down!" He yelled. Three more rats fell from the ceiling right on the kitchen table. Two charged from the front room on the floor at them. Sarah screamed, pushing herself down into the corner.

Her father charged. He moved perfectly, swinging the sword and dispatching the two on the floor. In the same motion, he effortlessly swung the sword, killing another on the table. It was a perfect technique, as he didn't scratch the floor or the table.

The two from the table jumped on the curtains as the one from the stairs hissed at them from the last step. More came from the ceiling and crawled above them as more came from the front room. Her father cut the curtain and kicked at another. Sarah covered her eyes in panic.

"Sarah, break for the basement!"

She couldn't move, hearing the sword swing in the air and rats hissing and skittering around her. The sounds they made were sickening when they were killed. Sarah screamed again when something grabbed her shoulder. It pulled her out of the corner hard. Her father swung the sword with his other hand, pulling her behind him. One scratched her right ankle as she ran with its claws. They ran up the stairs with at least seven following them.

"Come on!" her father urged, pulling her up the stairs.

"Get down," he ordered, kicking out at the ones following them. Sarah dropped to the butt, fear of whelming her mind.

She didn't see the rat that dropped from the ceiling, forcing them to stop being cut in half.

"Sarah," her dad pleaded, fighting hard, "get to the office."

Sarah was frozen in terror, shaking all over. Her joints were frozen, paralyzed, frantic with terror, her eyes clasped shut, covering her ears, striving to spare her the shrieks and screeches of the rats dying.

Between grunts and breaths of action, her dad pleaded, "Sarah, please, get out of here. I can't hold them forever."

Through the darkness beyond her closed eyes, a soft, warm light burned the darkness back. The light burned the black away and overpowered her panic. The new light danced in front of her as it grew. It cultivated until there was nothing else, as it overcame even where she was, and the danger taking over their home. The power and light of the amulet filled her and overflowed with strength.

As quick as a thought, faster than she could blink, she was off like a shot and discovered she was in the office. The shock had taken her breath away; it was and felt as easy as lifting a finger. Her hearing suddenly wrapped around her face as it caught up with her. Turning, gasping, she could see her father down the hall. She could see her father's upper half partway up the stairs, still fighting.

Her father hadn't seen her move but felt where she was with his leg as he backed away before he ran to be with her. He entered behind her, shut the door, and braced it with his weight behind it. Little bumps and scratches followed them all the way.

The light within her suddenly left her, bringing pain shooting up her leg and fear soaking her. Sarah fell to the floor, holding her ankle. There were squeaking noises from outside, and then claws were going up the door, the walls, and all around.

"How bad is it?" he asked, huffing, looking at her holding her ankle.

"I don't know, it just hurts." She groaned.

"We are safe until they try another way in," he said, examining his office for points of entry.

There was a whooshing sound from downstairs. Sarah's father pushed against the door again. Clattering and banging sounded from downstairs in the kitchen. Sarah moved away from the door as her father tightened his grip on the sword. Rats were squeaking as the scratching noise grew louder around them. Some are from downstairs, others from above them. They grew louder, and it sounded like dozens were in the hallway.

"Get ready!" he told Sarah as he moved his feet in anticipation, distancing himself from the door.

Then there was silence. Sarah opened one eye and then the other. "What are they doing?" she whispered.

"I don't know, just be ready for anything."

Silence. There was only the sound of their breathing as Sarah felt her heartbeat with her free hand.

"Knock, knock," came the sound on the door.

Sarah and her dad exchanged nervous looks. "Who is it?" he asked, placing the sword tip against the door. He was ready to push it through the center of the wood.

"Did someone order a pizza?"

It was her grandfather! "It's safe now."

Sarah adjusted her weight and limped gingerly on her right leg as her father opened the door. When her father opened it cautiously, they saw that it was the security guard from the school standing at the door, holding two pizzas and smiling.

"One cheese, one pepperoni, mushroom, and olive large dominos." He said happily.

"What, what happened to the rats?" Sarah gasped, stowing her piece of the amulet in her pocket.

"They were good," Renfield said, licking his lips and quickly moving down the hallway. "I am so glad you don't like garlic on your pizzas."

"You ate them?" Sarah examined, feeling like she was going to throw up.

"Well, there are only two pizzas here, and I never liked pepperoni, to say nothing of mushrooms and olives, yuk. Your father only had good taste in ladies."

They walked down the hall and the stairs with Sarah, supported by her father. Renfield laid the food on the table and looked out the window, taking a deep breath with a smile. His hair and face changed as he seemed to shrink. He was himself again, wearing a nice suit and coat.

"Just sit here," her father said, pulling a seat out for her. "I will get the bandages."

"I will keep a lookout," Renfield said, bobbing his head around.

Her father hurried upstairs as Sarah checked her leg. Four long cuts lined her leg and ankle. "Am I going to need stitches?"

"I don't know," Renfield said, still looking outside.

"Can you take a look at it?"

Renfield seemed to shiver. Taking a deep breath, his excited demeanor lessened as he lowered his head slightly. "I cannot," he said soberly. "My nature is delicate and must be balanced. Do not tempt me, I pray."

There was something in the way that he spoke that scared Sarah. The extra life that her grandfather had ebbed away, but didn't stop his head from moving.

"Here you go," her father said, descending the stairs. He had a bandage in his hand and disinfectant in the other. He treated her leg, and she winced from the sting of the ointment but didn't scream. She felt embarrassed because of how she acted over the past few minutes, and also kept that strange moment of super speed in the back of her mind.

"The police are on their way," Renfield said somberly.

"Here?" her father asked.

"No," Renfield said, turning his head up and straining his ear. "Down the street. Mrs. Dropleton apparently got it worse than we did and is missing several cats. That's just terrible."

Was he being sarcastic?

"Ok, try and stand on it."

She sat up and found that the pain was almost all gone. Her father smiled and put away the items he didn't use. She sat and felt strangely cold now that things were quiet. Her hands started to shake, but she didn't want to say anything. When her father returned, he had a flashlight and moved as if he were going to the basement. He stopped and put a hand on her shoulder.

"It's the adrenaline," he said softly. "It is wearing off. The shaking will stop soon. Get a blanket if you need one." Then he rose and said, "I'm going to check the wires."

"That's fine," Renfield said calmly, keeping a keen watch.

Her father left as she could hear sirens from far off. They both watched them pass and go by. Neither said anything as time passed. Sarah didn't feel like talking. She only sat and wished she had done better and understood more. The light over her head flickered and stayed on soon after her father appeared.

"Got them fixed for now. Those little buggers cut it in three places, and I thought the one under the hood stank. Pppwwww."

"So they didn't just come after us?" Sarah asked, holding her knees close to her chest in her chair.

"No," Renfield said. "It seems they are in a radius of twelve blocks to fifteen around us, or that is all I can sense."

"Looks like we are going to have to flush the pipes," her father said.

"Yep, we have a gofer," Renfield said, coming away from the window. "I don't think we will have any more trouble tonight."

"What did they want," Sarah asked. She felt like she was going to freak out.

"There is one key rat which has grown to control these others. They were sent out broadly, but when they are close, they can feel the power of the Telum Deos and will do all they can to destroy the one carrying it. I thought it was indestructible until I saw it split in four."

Sarah and her grandfather exchanged weary looks. "Don't you worry? Tomorrow, your grandfather and I will head out in the morning and take care of the leader."

"You will do what?" she asked.

"Sarah, this is what I have been doing since we got here, even before you were born."

Sarah's mind didn't want to work for some reason. She didn't even realize what she was told; nothing would have affected her more than what she was about to say.

"Can you teach me?"

"What?" her father said.

"Really?" Renfield asked excitedly.

"Can you teach me?" she asked again, still unable to understand what her voice said. "Can you teach me to use a sword and defend myself? Can I help?"

They all stayed where they were. Each was so different in mood than the other. Renfield cleared his throat, "Since you were able to liven a portion of the Telum Deos. We might have a chance if you can access even a portion of its power."

Her father sat down and put his head on the table, thinking. Renfield nodded toward Sarah and waved a hand, telling her to wait.

"Perhaps we can use some new blood in the family business?" he asked eagerly.

It took the longest time before her father raised his head and said, "Perhaps we can."

Perry was still feeling excited that their team had won the other day. He kept looking through his phone at all the pictures everyone had posted of the game as he walked to his father's class. Mondays were the worst, but what happened over the weekend made it more complicated. He didn't sleep much with all the animal control and police sirens going off through the night. Only a handful of students were left and lingered in the hallways now that school had ended. Several kids said hello as he passed them in the hall. He stopped walking and checked the hallway before entering his father's classroom. Above the door was a sign, "Mr. Holmwood."

"Hello, Father," Perry said, checking around the classroom to see if they were alone.

"Son, how are you." Mr. Holmwood said warmly.

"Great," he said, moving some things off his father's desk and sat down. His father was busy looking through some cabinets. Mr. Holmwood had the most organized, cluttered classroom in the school.

"We won the game, and the surprise guests were amazing," Perry said, still swiping through the pictures. "Too bad you missed it."

"Not that." Mr. Holmwood said. His voice carried with it a darkness that wasn't there before.

"Oh," Perry said in surprise. He jumped up and stood straight. "The incursion went as we anticipated, but what was strange was that there were several encounters of what didn't appear to be normal resistance."

Mr. Holmwood left his cabinets with some folders in his hands. "Working with these small amounts of resources is almost intolerable. All these moments long for the days when darkness was so much more prominent and controllable. The information we can gather from those small vermin can't even let us know one from several."

"At least it was fun." Perry shrugged.

"These conflicting results are of no matter," Mr. Holmwood said, placing his files in an old briefcase. "Our time is coming, and we are getting closer. We have work to do."

He took his son under his arm as they left the classroom, turning off the lights. "Let us go have more fun." He said to his son, shutting the door and widening his smile.

www.ingramcontent.com/pod-product-compliance
Lightning Source LLC
Chambersburg PA
CBHW020808310726

48969CB00002B/763